Skinner At The International

During the 1950's the author worked as a window cleaner on buildings in Minneapolis and St. Paul, Minnesota, Chicago, Illinois, Spokane, Washington and elsewhere.

Although the setting is the Twin Cities, events described in this book occurred in various cities around the country.

This book is a work of fiction and is based partly on incidents which took place in the life of the author.

Any resemblance to persons living or dead is strictly coincidental. The locale is the state of Minnesota and is not intended to be an accurate representation of places or geographic locations. It is used for background only.

Thanks to Lois Lonnquist and Mike Logan
for their assistance in editing.

Front Cover design by Del Lonnquist

International Standard Book Number
ISBN   0-9786963-3-6

For information contact: skinner@MtSky.com

Skinner At The International

By Del Lonnquist

This book is dedicated to
my wife Lois who worked hard
to help me make it through Brown Institute.
And in memory of Richard and Helen Brown,
who helped so many thousands of us enter
the world of broadcasting with their school,
The American Institute of The Air,
which became Brown Institute
and then Brown College

Skinner At The International
By Del Lonnquist

We may not live in the past, but the past lives in us.
Sam Pisar - Holacaust Survivor

Chapter One – The Beginning

I was hanging by the safety belt, feet in front of my face. I couldn't breathe. The fall had knocked the breath out of me. My head hurt and I had a sharp pain in my side. I was staring down at the garbage cans and junk in the alley five and a half floors below. Dazed, it took a moment before I realized where I was and what had happened. I was cleaning a window on the sixth floor of the bank building when I slipped and fell.

The fall had taken place many years ago, but the memory, when it returned was as real as the fall had been then. Twenty five years had passed. I was a small town radio news reporter, not a window cleaner on the buildings in St. Paul, Minnesota. I had been invited to a news conference at the White House with a dozen other small town reporters.

It was February; dirty slush had built up along the curbs of the nation's capital. A drab dreary day in Washington D.C., but to the dozen news people gathered in the Cabinet Room it was anything but dreary. The air of expectancy was a tangible thing in the room as reporters waited for the big moment of their day in Washington. The White House staff had provided background briefings on everything going on in government. Reporters attending the news conference received enough material to fill a good many small town newspapers and radio newscasts.

The reporters rose swiftly to their feet as an aide announced "Ladies and Gentlemen, the President of the United States," and Jimmie Carter walked through the door. As the news people were seated he brought a quick laugh while apologizing for the absence of Jody Powell his Press Secretary. "Jody," the President said, "is out of town conducting migratory waterfowl population density surveys this week."

As a dozen or so heads nodded wisely, the President broke into a toothy grin, "He's duck hunting. He's duck hunting," he said, obviously pleased with himself that he had tossed the news people a zinger. He then gave a brief report on the Camp David Peace Talks and called for questions.

For some reason I couldn't think of any.

Others at the table were soon asking questions about foreign affairs and domestic policies. The president brightened as he responded to each question. Looking them in the eye as he began his answer, the president had no trouble commanding the attention of every small town reporter.

Still in awe of the surroundings I looked around the room as the President talked. He commented on the Camp David Peace Accords and peace among peoples of diverse colors and ethnic backgrounds.

As he spoke about people of all nations learning to live together, I thought back to my days with Mexican Joe, Black Bill, Orbit the Polish Kid, Czech from Czechoslovakia, Sir Winston from England, Ooftuh the Norwegian, Chippewa Charlie from a northern Minnesota reservation, and all the others who made up the crew of the International Window Cleaning Company of The Twin Cities.

We called it The International.

It wasn't just the company name. It was the makeup of the crew and their ethnic heritage.

It was the early 50's. Light years away from this richly paneled and carpeted room in the White House.

As President Carter talked about his hopes for peace between people of all colors and ethnic backgrounds I thought of the morning bull session when Frank the Boss introduced me to his crew.

"Hey guys, here's a new man. Says he knows how to clean windows, says he's a building man. Joe, take'm out and see what he can do on the outside of a tall building."

Some of the crew stepped forward, with a "Hey Skinner, welcome to The International." The pride they had in the company was obvious, and the salutation, "Skinner," meant that I was a probationary member of the crew. If everything worked out, I would be accepted as a full-fledged window cleaner, a member of the crew, someone they could trust with their life. A skinner, in window cleaners parlance was a guy who looked at a window, decided it was clean enough, and "skinned" by, leaving it until the next scheduled cleaning.

I had cleaned windows in Minneapolis, St. Paul, Chicago and other cities. From coast to coast, wherever you worked for a window cleaning company you were "Skinner" until they knew whether you would really work or just skin by. Before Joe and I could leave for the first job I had to be checked out by the oldest man on the crew. They called him Czech. He had immigrated from Czechoslovakia right after the war. According to Harry the Cat, Czech had drifted through several camps filled with thousands of refugees waiting for repatriation or resettlement in another country. Like so many of the people who lost home and family during the second war to end all wars, he set his aim on America, where he was sure he would find streets of gold.

"Lonnquist," he said, "Lonnquist, you ain't a herring choker are you?" I looked around to see if he was pulling my leg but nobody laughed. "Whatta ya mean, herring choker?" I mumbled.
I guess he didn't know whether I was smarting off, or if I was really so dumb I didn't know what a herring choker was.

"Whatta ya mean, what do I mean," growled Czech, "are you a Herring Choker or ain't ya?"

Joe said, "Hey Mister Del, is your father a Swede or ain't he?"
I'd been called Ole, Snoose, Dumb Swede, and a lot of other names but this was a first.

Herring choker, what the heck was that all about? "Well what about it kid, is your old man a Swede or ain't he?" asked Czech.
"Well yeah but I ain't never seen him eat a herring," I offered as a defense for my ignorance.

"All right, all right," Frank the Boss said, "we don't care what he is. It's what he does that counts. Now let's get this show on the road."

"Okay Joe," said Czech, "Find out if Herring Choker knows the difference between a brush and a sponge. But keep an eye on him, he probably won't find his way back to the shop if he loses sight of you."

So Herring Choker it was, and Herring Choker it stayed as long as I worked at what was a United Nations of Window Cleaning Companies.

The United Nations was a pretty new thing in the early fifties and we didn't really understand the lofty goals of The Great Lady, as we called Eleanor Roosevelt.

All we knew was that the United Nations and Trygvie Lee it's Secretary General were supposed to stop war, erase famine, and bring a better life to everyone. People of all different races and nationalities were supposed to start getting along better.

At the International, there didn't seem to be that problem. Everyone was just trying to get by, make a living and take care of themselves. Take care of their families, if they had one.

Stay off welfare or survive one more night in a skid row flop house if that was their life style.

Life just didn't seem as hard to understand in those few years' right after the war.

There seemed to be someone of every race and color at the International. All had nick names that described them and their ethnic heritage. And they all seemed to get along. Some lived in real homes with real families. Many were denizens of the skid row areas of the Twin Cities and weren't above doing a little panhandling during the noon hour when crowds were biggest. Some were winos, drunks and scam artists, wise in the ways of the streets. They worked when they needed to and had found a home at The International.

Besides Mexican Joe and Czech, there was Black Bill, Ooftuh the Norwegian and Blind Bob, whose nationality didn't seem to matter. He had lost most of the sight in one eye and some in the other as a child. Despite the loss of vision he could clean windows as well or better than any man on the crew. The names they called one another may not have been considered politically correct according to today's culture, but it seemed to give everyone on the crew of the International an identity. A sense of belonging, of being connected somehow to their heritage and ancestral roots through the names they were called by their coworkers.

Chapter Two - The Fall
This is the first step toward becoming better than you are. Julius Charles

I would never forget the first step on the road from the International, with its skid row denizens, to a news conference in the cabinet room at the White House with its leather chairs, richly paneled walls and the group of well-dressed reporters I was with.

The first step was actually the fall from the sixth floor of the old Empire Bank building on Robert Street in downtown St. Paul. That was the day this 25 year journey began.

After all these years I can remember every detail, close my eyes and relive every moment as if it were taking place today.

I was cleaning windows on the backside of the old brick building. The windows looked down on the alley. It was hot, a spring day in late May. The wind coming off the river was funneling up between the buildings on Robert Street. It always seemed to blow harder as it swirled its way through the alleys of downtown. Little dust eddy's were blowing up from the sand piles that the winter storms had left in the corners of the buildings and the cracks in the sidewalks. Sand that city crews had spread on snow covered streets throughout the winter.

Grime from the smoke of a thousand oil and coal burning furnaces coated the window ledges of the taller buildings. As the water and detergent we used to clean the windows, combined with the winters smoky residue it made the window sills slick.

We all knew we had to make sure safety belts were firmly locked onto the small bolts which stuck out on each side of the windows. The first wasps of the season were beginning to buzz around us as we worked the sunny sides of the buildings. Wasps were an occupational hazard, unless you were Mexican Joe, who always joked about them and just brushed them off when they landed on his arms.

Having been stung a few times in the past I was a bit wary of them.

This day I was on the outside with my partner Lars Larsen, or Ooftuh, as everyone called him, on the inside. I was doing cross overs.

Stepping from one window to the next, working my way across the outside of the old building.

Frank the Boss always told us, "Don't do crossovers. Go in and out of each window. Better safe than sorry. Don't take chances!"

But it saved time and was a lot easier to just step from one window to the next on the outside while your building partner went from window to window on the inside. Doing crossovers meant that it was not necessary to open and close the old windows which on most of the buildings had been painted so many times they frequently stuck in their grooves. They were hard to push up and down, sometimes nearly impossible. We saved a lot of time and energy with one person inside and the other outside.

This time I had a problem and didn't know it. My partner, Ooftuh, got a few windows ahead and decided to take a 3.2 beer break at the bar just around the corner on Robert Street. Since I didn't drink beer, he didn't bother telling me he was leaving. I was working alone but didn't know it.

There I was in the middle of the crossover, one side of my safety rope hooked to the bolt sticking out of the wall by one window and the brass buckle on other end of the rope about to be fastened to the bolts on the next window. I was holding on to a corner brick and stretching out as far as I could to step across the space between the two windows.

A wasp buzzed past my head. I let go of the brick to brush it away. In a split second I was flying off the side of the building. I hit the end of the safety rope and slammed into the side of the building several feet below the window, five and a half floors in the air.

When I came to a few seconds later I was hanging by the leather belt strapped around my waist. My feet were in front of my face. I couldn't breathe. My head hurt, I had a sharp pain in my side and I was staring down at the alley five and a half floors below. Dazed, it took a moment before I realized where I was and what had happened.

That's when the fear hit. Like a jolt of electricity.

I froze. My stomach tied in a knot.

It took a minute or two before I could get it through my head that I had fallen off the building and was now hanging upside down five and a half floors above the alley. This was real. If I was going to get back up to the window I had so recently climbed out of I had to do something fast. I reached above my head and grabbed the rope.

One of the office workers who had been watching me clean the window said he never saw anyone come up a rope that fast.

As I climbed I remember my eyes staring at the rusty old bolt sticking out of the wall and at the brass hook on the end of my safety rope which was attached to the old bolt. If I jerked on the rope and put too much pressure on it would it come out of the wall? If I pulled too hard would the end break off and send me flying toward the ground?

We all knew that some of the bolts we hooked our safety belts onto were unsafe and that occasionally a bolt would loosen up and pull right out of the wall.

The older crew members said insurance companies considered you dead if you fell from five floors or above.

Would it hold? If the bolt did let go could I survive the fall? These were the questions racing through my mind as I went racing up the rope.

I climbed on to the window ledge and reaching behind me grabbed the loose end of my safety rope and hooked on to the bolt on the other side of the window.

Several office workers were staring at the window frozen in place. Seeing an apparition that had first disappeared from the window, and then moments later reappeared climbing up the rope. I tried to open the window but couldn't get a good grip on it and motioned for one of the office workers to open it.

No one moved.

It was as if they were too stunned to comprehend what I needed of them. After what seemed like an eternity the office boy ran to the window and grasping the handles on the bottom pulled it open.

I tried to say thanks while climbing in but could hardly talk.

I just stuttered.

I tried to light a smoke and my hands were shaking so bad the cigarettes flew out of them and scattered on the floor. The office boy picked one up and lit it for me.

The whole thing lasted only a few short minutes but the nightmare that resulted lasted for many years.

I would wake up in the middle of the night in a cold sweat.

Falling.

The fall from the building lasted only a few seconds and ended when I slammed against the brick wall, the fall in my dreams lasted for years. It never seemed to end. In the dream I would fall and fall until I finally woke up short of breath, shaking and wringing wet. Many years passed before the dreams came less often and began to fade away.

Although I didn't realize it at the time my career as a radio broadcaster was about to begin.

Arriving home from work I told my wife Lois about the fall.

"I didn't get my safety belt hooked up right and fell from the sixth floor of the Empire Bank!

I was still nervous and excited about the fall and anxious to tell someone about it.

But she said, "That settles it. You're going back to school!"

I could tell by the tone in her voice that night school for radio announcing was going to be a reality.

Despite having two kids and not enough money to go around I would go. She was serious and would make this happen.

We had talked about it. I had dreamed about becoming a radio announcer but there were always reasons to put it off. Good reasons.

I had played guitar with a country road band and thought making music was the greatest way to make a living there was. But traveling on the road with a band was not easy when you had a family. Being a Dee Jay and playing music on the air was the next best thing to actually creating the music.

The time just never seemed right to take the big plunge and enroll at The American Institute of the Air, which was the radio broadcasting school on Lake Street in Minneapolis.

We always needed the money for the kids, or one of them would get sick. There was always a reason to put off school.

Until now.

Until a flop from a window as the other members of the crew called it, gave school and a career in broadcasting a much higher priority. It wasn't going to be easy. We knew that but it would take more than a lack of money to stop us. We were on our way.

Lois got a job as a waitress. I continued working days as a window cleaner and weekends doing janitor work in apartment buildings. That's the way we made night school for radio announcing happen.

That was the moment we began the trek which carried us first to WMIQ Radio in Iron Mountain, Michigan then to stations in Minnesota, Wisconsin, Florida and Montana. It eventually brought me to the White House and this news conference with the President of The United States.

It started as I told her about the fall from the sixth floor of the old bank building. It started when she looked around and saw the trailer house we lived in, the two small children, and when she saw ahead a lifetime of worry about when and where the next fall would be. That's the moment radio announcers school became a reality.

As I listened to the president, and looked around the room at the other news people, I lived once again, "the fall."

Chapter Three - The Hungarian

*A man cannot free himself from the past more easily
than he can free himself from his own body. André Maurois*

President Carter was seated three feet away at the end of the table.
He talked at length about the lack of human rights in some countries and
how the world needed to change.

Memories carried me back to the 1950's and the Hungarian refugee
who had become a skinner at the International.

Hungk, as he was called, had suffered far more injustice during those
few years before, during and after the second war to end all wars than any
one man should have to endure in a lifetime. And all of his suffering
didn't seem to have changed the world even a little bit.

It just took him down.

He suffered from the results of those injustices for all the days of his
booze shortened life.

Like so many others he had immigrated to the United States after, The
War, as we called World War Two in those days, as if it was going to be
the only one we'd ever have to fight.

His arms were always covered by a shirt with long sleeves, even on the
hottest days of summer.

Some of the guys gave him a hard time about it and razzed him about
being cold blooded and stuff like that.

Then one day Frank the Boss spread the word that it was not a matter
to joke about. He said, "Lay off the Hungarian and let him do his job."

Frank told Czech later, Hungk had numbers on his arms that had been
tattooed on in the Nazi concentration camps during the war.

Hungk showed Czech those despised numbers during one of their late
night drinking sprees. Showed him the terrible scars on his arm from the
time he tried to burn the hated death camp numbers off while on a long
weekend drunk.

During an evening of hard drinking he had torn open the sleeves of his
shirt, poured whiskey on the hated reminders of his imprisonment, and
set the whiskey on fire with a match.

He had then taken a lit cigarette and tried to burn each tiny number off with the red hot, burning tobacco.

The numbers, tattooed into the skin on his arms, survived even that painful assault. They were a daily reminder of the most terrifying days, and the saddest moments of his life. These were memories from which he could not escape, even with the help of his ever present bottle of Muscatel wine.

I guess when you give somebody a hard time because they're different, you never really know why it is they do the things that make them seem different.

Hungk, like the rest of the crew of the International, was different, no question about that. Maybe that's why we all got along so well. We were different, and nobody wondered why. Everyone just accepted it.

The Hungarian was normally a quiet man, given to heavy drinking, and dark brooding periods.

One night when he and Czech were really pouring it down he began talking about his life during the war. Czech said later he started to talk about what happened to his sister when the Germans came, but he had broken down and cried before he could relate much of the story. He couldn't seem to get it out of his mind.

I suppose now they'd call it post traumatic something or other and would do something for him but no one knew what to do about it then.

Once I walked into a room where he was cleaning venetian blinds and saw him standing there just staring at his arm. His long sleeved shirt covered it completely, yet his eyes were locked on the spot where the hated numbers lay, hidden by the blue chambray material.

I could tell from the faraway look in his eyes that he wasn't seeing the shirt sleeve. He was viewing something far beyond what was visible to me, something far away from my world, but which seemed to encompass all of his.

I turned so I could slip out the door, afraid to interrupt whatever pictures the thought of those terrible numbers were bringing to him.

He heard the scrape of my boot on the concrete floor and swung quickly around with a fierce look on his face and murder in his eyes.

The words he spat out in that scary moment were in a language I had no knowledge of but his expression, and his actions were all too clear.

He slowly returned to the present with a shudder that started in his shoulders and seemed to move through his entire body.

Without another word; he put down his tools and headed for the door.

I knew we wouldn't be seeing the Hungarian anytime soon.

Czech said he was drunk for a week.

When he was in a particularly dark time, like the day he hid in the second basement of the Northern Pacific Railroad building and didn't come out all day, everybody sort of looked away and made small talk about the St. Paul Saints or Minneapolis Millers, until Frank got there to take him home.

One day we were working on the Central Pacific Railroad Building or the CP as it was called and were taking a mid-morning break in the third sub-basement.

The Hungarian bought a coke, poured half of it down the drain in the sink and filled the bottle on up to the top with the alcohol we put in the water to keep it from freezing in the winter.

He sat down on one end of a work bench and in his thick, guttural accent said "So long kid, see you at quitting time," shook the concoction up and down a couple of times then chug-a-lugged the whole bottle.

He started leaning backward to lie down and was out before his head hit the bench top.

At quitting time when we couldn't wake him somebody called an ambulance. It didn't do any good.

He never opened his eyes again.

It was a cold and lonely place to give up your life, the third sub-basement of the old CP Building.

A concrete tomb that echoed with every step you took, and every word you said. A dark, dreary, dungeon of a place, lit by a few bare incandescent light bulbs hanging from the steel ceiling beams that held back the real world.

This was a subterranean world occupied on a strictly temporary basis, by janitors, and people who needed to store or unstore material needed in the real world that began three floors above.

A lowly world vacated by most people as quickly as possible. Occupied briefly by people who never seemed to speak out loud because of the echoes which reverberated with every word.

For Hungk, it proved to be the end of the world as he knew it.

A concrete tunnel that hopefully, had the light of a better world at its end. Mexican Joe said "it's probably just as well, because Hungk had bad spirits in his mind from what happened to his sister and parents during the war. This may have been the only way he could find rest."

We decided he was probably right because Joe was sort of religious and often said, "Hail Mary Mother of Jesus," and other religious stuff.

Seems like a lot of us get so bottled up inside our problems that we just can't seem to find our way out again.

The Hungarian didn't have any relatives that we knew about, no wife, no kids and no friends except Czech who did a lot of boozing with him. There was no money for a funeral, but someone called the morgue to find out when they were going to bury him out at The Ridges. That's the cemetery where they plant the folks who have no one to do their funeral.

We borrowed a couple of the company trucks and went out there but didn't really know what to do. It was a bright sunny day, and that only seemed to bring out the drabness of the Hungarians final resting place.

What had, at one time, been bushes to separate this dreary burying ground of the poor from the rest of the world, were now scraggly, leafless, weed filled brambles.

Located on the hill from which the cemetery drew its name, and overlooking the river bottoms, the Ridges, was a drab, dreary place. The Mississippi could be seen in the distance, through the haze and smoke of the nearby factories, and petroleum plants.

The Hungarian went to his grave in a place as cheerless as the walk up rooms he had lived in all those years since the war.

Mexican Joe said a couple of Hail Mary's, and talked a little about Purgatory. The rest of us sort of looked around without really looking at each other and were glad when it was over. The crew from the morgue cracked a couple of jokes about how this was the biggest funeral crowd they had ever seen on "Boot Hill," as they called their workplace.

Joe thought we should try and pray him into Heaven or something, but we all figured Hungk was already wherever it was he was supposed to go.

Besides, the rest of the crew was ready to, as Jamie Kennedy put it, "head for the Pigs Eye Saloon and hoist one to the memory of the dearly departed." As quickly as possible, but without appearing to hurry, everyone climbed into the company trucks and headed off to the Pigs Eye. This was the downtown, just-below-the-loop tavern frequented by most of the crew of the International.

The Hungarian had occupied the dimly lit, smoke filled, back booth of the Pigs Eye on many a night. It was a fitting place for his fellow Skinners to "hoist one" in his memory

Chapter Four - The Browns

The world should know how wonderful these people were.

As the President answered questions from the small town reporters, he talked about the need for people to help one another. There was a need for people to work together and to help the nation get over what he called "the national malaise."

He spoke of the need to restore the nation's greatness through government programs that would help people to help themselves and encourage them to help one another. As he spoke, I thought of the people who had helped me along the way.

It seemed like such a long, long time since that spring night I had walked up the stairs to The American Institute of the Air at 3123 East Lake Street in Minneapolis and applied for admission to the school which trained radio announcers.

Helen Brown, who with her husband Richard had founded the school, sat across the desk from me and asked questions about my background, education, or lack of it, since I was a high school dropout. Only in those days you didn't "drop out" of school, you just quit. Years later the high mucky mucks found the euphemism "drop out" to make it sound better.

The world may have seen an uneducated young man who had quit school and worked as a window cleaner and janitor to support his family, but Helen Brown said she saw, a radio announcer.

After I had read some news and several commercials for her as an audition, Mrs. Brown looked across the desk and in her soft voice, with its controlled enunciation, said, "Mr. Lonnquist, you read very well, I believe you are going to be a good radio announcer."

I couldn't believe what I was hearing. They were accepting me into the school. She called me Mister, a title we reserved for the high mucky mucks in whose offices we cleaned the windows. No matter that I had quit school and didn't have a lot of money. She thought I could be an announcer. The door to a new world had opened a small crack, and the opportunity to step through was just ahead. It was a moment I would never forget.

As she stood to terminate the interview I saw for the first time the crutches at her side and the steel braces on her twisted legs. In those days they meant only one thing. Polio.

Mrs. Brown had polio and was physically handicapped but I hadn't realized it until she stood up.

It was then that she called to her husband Richard Brown, the founder of the school, to come in from his office to welcome the new student.

As the door opened, his crutches came through the door first, followed by his polio twisted legs. The infirmities of those crippled legs were obscured by the size of the welcoming smile which was big and open. It was obvious that this man had overcome any handicaps of the body he had, and was now ready to help those of us whose handicaps, although not of a physical nature, were just as real, if not so readily discernible.

The president talked about helping others achieve their goals and helping others reach out for their share of the American Dream. I couldn't help but think back to Helen and Richard Brown who in their lifetimes helped so many thousands of young people. They had changed the course of thousands of lives; not only through their school, but through the example they set in their daily lives.

I suppose the average person would have to live several lifetimes to do as much for others as Helen and Richard Brown did in their 53 years together.

They opened their school a couple of years after World War Two and called it The American Institute of the Air. The school was housed in two small second floor rooms above a drug store on the corner of Nicolet and Lake in Minneapolis. As the years went by they expanded until it covered several buildings farther down Lake Street and was called Brown Institute. Still later it became Brown College. Theirs was a triumph of spirit and will over the frailties of the body. They were an inspiration to every young person who carried within themselves the dream of being a broadcaster.

I started school the following Monday evening and for Lois and me it was the opening lap of a fifty year ride.

Chapter Five - Harry The Cat

It is only in adventure that some people
succeed in finding themselves. André Gide

The reporters gathered for the news conference with the President seemed to be a cross section of small town newsrooms. As varied as the newspapers and radio stations they represented. From South Dakota ranch country to the suburbs of New York and Boston.

It was almost like going back in time to the morning bull session at The International.

Like the reporters, the men who made up the crew of the International, seemed to have come from every imaginable background. Small towns to big cities.

There was Harry the Cat, for example. He told everyone who would listen, that in his younger days, he had been a cat man, a human fly, able to climb up the side of a building by hanging onto the bricks with his fingertips.

Back in the 20's, as he often told us, he had been a flagpole sitter in New York and down the coast to Florida. He had even climbed up the side of the old Laurel Hotel in St. Paul, all 15 stories, one brick at a time.

Harry resented getting old, and would sometimes climb out a window several floors above the city sidewalks without hooking his safety belt. Out of sheer defiance he would clean the window without the required safety equipment. Standing on the inches wide ledge and hanging on with his fingertips to the center of the window.

Harry was of diminutive stature, barely hitting five foot four, and had greasy looking gray hair that always looked as though it had been a week or two away from the last washing. He was otherwise what the old timers referred to as a "Dapper Dan." He would periodically dampen his finger tips and run them down what passed for a crease in his faded gray work pants, in a vain effort to make them look pressed. He was from the old school of workers who tried to, "act the gentleman," as Czech put it, especially if we were working in an office with ladies present.

Harry was always proving to himself, and anyone working with him, that he was just as good a man as when he was young.

With a defiant look in his eye, and with shoulders squared, he would climb out a window several floors up in the air, without hooking up his safety belt.

The day he took a flop off the third floor of the old WCC0 Radio building on Third Street in Minneapolis cured him of that though.

It was one of those rare times when he actually did wear the safety belt which Frank insisted he take when he left the shop in the morning. The leather safety belt with large brass buckles had a leather loop sewed and riveted to the back. The safety rope with brass buckles on the ends slid through the loop on the back of the belt and kept the rope even with your waist while you cleaned the windows.

Instead of tying a knot in the end of the long rope to adjust its length to the different sized windows, Harry left the rope so long that everybody could see he wore it only because Frank and the insurance company demanded it. Harry had his safety belt hooked on both sides of the window the day he slipped and fell so he only dropped a few feet. The long rope hooked to the bolts sticking out of the wall on each side of the window caught him just as his chin hit the window ledge he had been standing on seconds earlier.

When his chin struck the brick ledge his false teeth were knocked out of his mouth and fell to the sidewalk three floors below. He wasn't bad hurt, but he was bruised, embarrassed, and mad. Boy was he mad!

It was during the heat of a humid, sweltering Minnesota summer afternoon, with heat waves rising off the streets of the city, that Harry The Cat tried one last time to live out his dream, to become once again the cat man of his youth. It was Blind Bob who spotted him inching his way up the corner of the Laurel Hotel on the corner of Fifth and Robert.

Harry had talked many times about the day back in the twenties when he had climbed all fifteen stories of the Laurel, one brick at a time.

Now, on the hottest day of the year, and after several hours of planning in the back booth of the Pigs Eye Saloon, Harry was reliving the days he talked about so much.

You just don't see a lot of human flies, as they were called in the old days, climbing up the side of a building. These were a strange breed of people who saw a building as an urban mountain that had to be climbed.

Harry was indeed a relic of days long gone.

Yet there he was, inching his way past the third floor of the old hotel when Blind Bob first saw him from his vantage point across the street at the old bank building.

He quickly climbed in the window and reached for a phone to call Frank, then dashed for the stairs and headed across the street.

Spotting Clyde and Czech working a truck route, he shouted for them to follow, then ran for the main desk in the hotel lobby.

Explaining what was happening he told the startled manager he needed keys to corner rooms from the fourth floor up, and that they should call the police and fire departments fast.

An assistant manager with keys in hand, and with Clyde and Czech close behind, headed for the fourth floor corner room where they threw open the window to await the coming of the cat man.

The windows were far enough from the corner that they were unable to reach Harry and could only talk with him, which proved to be singularly unsuccessful.

Harry was living out his dream. He had done it when he was young and he could do it now. He could climb the Laurel, brick by brick, all the way to the top.

It was while he was slowly inching his way past the fourth floor that police with bullhorns ordered him to come down, and that's when Frank the Boss made his appearance too.

"Harry, listen to me Harry. This is crazy, it's too hot. You're not as young as you were when you did this before. Listen to me Harry. Stay where you are and let us get a rope out to you."

No response from the gray haired old man whose full concentration seemed to be on every brick he touched. He was doing it. He was climbing the building, one brick at a time. Pressing in with arms and legs, and with the soles of his shoes seeking out each little niche between the bricks, Harry the Cat was once again "The Cat Man - The Human Fly." He was doing it again.

Apparently several hours of trying to cool off at The Pig's Eye Saloon had given him just enough, "Jack Daniels Courage" as some called it, to get him started on his quest.

The crew of the International with police and firemen close behind headed for the fifth floor where again they awaited his arrival.

Police issued orders to come in, Frank pleaded, Clyde and Blind Bob tried to come up with a plan.

TV news crews were filming, a couple of radio stations were doing live reports, a crowd gathered in the street below, and firemen on the ground prepared a huge net which they moved close to the building blocking the sidewalk.

Brick by brick, inch by inch, the old man made his way slowly, cautiously toward the top of the old building.

At each floor the windows were thrown open, and the police, firemen, Frank and the crew of the International would lean out and try in vain to get him to stop his climb.

At the eleventh floor he seemed to be weakening and for a moment it seemed that he would give up the quest, but then with a long look toward the top, now only four floors above, he started up again.

At floor twelve it was obvious he was through. Sweat was beaded on his forehead and had soaked through his shirt.

The break in Harry's concentration came as Frank said quietly "Come in now Harry, you've shown everybody you can still do it, come in now."

Sweat poured from his face, his chest heaved with the exertion, and for the first time the exhausted old man looked over toward his friends in the window.

As he did, Frank said "Give it up Harry, we'll help you in. Let us give you a hand."

"It's no use, I can't make it Frank," Harry whispered in a gasping voice. "I can't make it. I told'em I climbed it once, and they laughed at me. Said I was just an old has been windbag. I had to show'em Frank, I had to show'em I'm a climber." With a voice reduced to a whisper by the strain he said, "help me in Frank, I can't hold on much longer, please Frank, help me in."

Turning to the crew Frank said "What are we gonna do guys, what can we do to reach him?"

"I think I have an idea Frank," said Clyde, and taking the long rope from the window cleaning belt he had carried with him he said, "Bob, you get out the window on that wall and I'll get in this one on the other wall. I'll throw the end of the rope around the corner of the building to you and we'll pull it tight and hold him against the wall until the fire department can get ladders up to him."

Bob climbed out the window and hooked up his safety belt putting him even with, but still seven or eight feet away from Harry. Clyde climbed half out the window on the other wall, braced himself with one leg hooked around the pipe on the radiator and the other gripping the outside of the building wall. He swung the rope back and forth several times before shouting "Here it comes Bob," and with a mighty heave, swung it around the corner toward the outstretched hands of his cohort. The rope missed the waiting hands by several feet and Bob shouted, "Higher Clyde, get it up higher, get it up higher, and stretch it out a couple of more feet."

Clyde again swung the rope back and forth several times in an ever widening arc, while the cat man, clinging to the bricks on either side of the building corner whispered, "Help me Frank, I can't hold on, I'm losing my grip Frank, I'm losing my grip."

With a mighty heave, Clyde threw the rope again. It seemed to sail as it flew slowly up and then around the corner of the building, with the middle of the long rope striking Harry the Cat squarely in the middle of the back, and the brass plated end piece continuing around the corner toward Bob's waiting hands. Bob leaned far to his left, arms stretched to their limits, mentally willing the rope to get longer, just two more inches, even one more inch. With a desperate look in his eye, while standing on the narrow three inch window ledge 12 floors in the air, he threw himself outward toward the rope with its small brass buckle. The end of the rope seemed to slow in its course and then to stop its forward movement altogether. Again, the brass buckle had moved tantalizingly near only to fall inches short of the outstretched hands. The rope paused in its flight. So still it stood.

Then slowly began its downward path brushing the sweat soaked shirt sleeve of the fast weakening old man It paused its flight for a split second as it touched him, then ever so slowly, it fell away.

In his weakened state, it was enough. It caused that arm to relax its grip on the brick for a split second, placing an even greater strain on the other arm and the tired old legs.

Harry's eyes never left Frank's, and in a voice suddenly calm, he said quietly "I'm a goner Frank, I'm a goner." As the crew looked on the old hands loosened their grip on the bricks, and from the twelfth floor, without another sound, Harry The Cat fell.

The net wasn't even close; he landed in the middle of the street with screaming people pushing and shoving to get out of the way.

It was a shaken group of men who made their way slowly down the stairs and out the massive oak doors of the old hotel into the stifling heat of a Minnesota dog days afternoon.

"Derelict Falls From Building," read the banner headline in the next morning's edition of the St. Paul Post Newspaper. The story was filled out with details supplied to reporters by police and fire officials. It told about the old man who had visited the Pig's Eye Saloon and after being taunted by others in the bar tried to climb to the top of the old hotel by clinging to the bricks on the corner of the structure.

"Derelict! They called Harry the Cat a derelict." shouted Czech during the morning bull session.

"We gotta set'em straight. Somebody's gotta to go to the paper and let'em know that Harry the Cat wasn't a derelict, he was a climber He was a real human fly. Somebody's gotta tell'em."

Clyde looked at me and said, "C'mon kid, you know how to talk to people. You go over to the paper and give'em the scoop on Harry, and take these clippings with you so they can see who Harry really was."

With that Clyde brought over a packet of yellowed newspaper clippings he had retrieved from Harry's room during the night. Clippings that dated back to the twenties showed a young, handsome, smiling Harry the Cat climbing skyscrapers in New York, and sitting on a flag pole in Miami. Harry the Cat had indeed been a "climber" in the twenties. A daredevil who would scale anything he could get a grip on.

He just might have been the last of the human flies.

"Okay, I'll go, but you and Czech have to come along to answer the questions they're going to ask about Harry."

And so we went, Big Clyde, Czech and I to find the reporter who wrote the story calling Harry the Cat a derelict.

They stopped us at the reception desk, looking askance at this group of window cleaners with our unkempt appearance. The receptionist made sharp inquiries as to our business at the paper. It was only after we showed the newspaper clippings of Harry the Cat in his youth that she finally called the newsroom to ask the reporter who wrote the story to come to the lobby.

After an initial show of skepticism, the reporter looked through the small bundle of clippings and called the City Editor.

"I think we've got a story Chief," said the young reporter, "about the old guy that fell from the Laurel yesterday. His friends are here and it turns out the old man really was one of those people who climbed up the sides of buildings. A human fly they call him. They said he had climbed all the way to the top of the Laurel thirty years ago, should I go with it?"

The front page of the St. Paul paper the next morning carried a full story, with pictures of Clyde and Czech, and a young Harry the Cat sitting on a flag pole high above the crowd. Here was a story that would have put Harry on cloud nine. It told of an old man who had tried to relive a dream. A man with fingers of steel, who knew no fear, and only wanted to prove it to the doubters of his present world.

Two days later we made the trip to the Ridges, where they buried the poor, the people who had no one to take care of their funeral expenses. We all went once again in company trucks. Gulls from the nearby river circled and squawked overhead observing this strange looking group. We watched county employees bury Harry the Cat in the traditional pine box.

He had lived out his dreams climbing man made mountains of brick and steel. He had lived on small platforms mounted on the very top of tall flag poles while spectators with queasy stomachs wondered how he could stand to be up so high.

Was it a coincidence? Or was it fate that they buried the human fly on the very top of the knoll that marked the high point of the Ridges?

A final salute to an old man who couldn't forget the halcyon days of a bygone era. He would now be on the highest point in the area, forever.

Had he been born to the aristocracy, Harry The Cat would have climbed the world's highest mountains. Lacking the trappings and advantages of the high mucky mucks of the world, he settled instead for the glitz and glitter of the promoters, who kept him climbing on man-made mountains, the steel and brick structures which brought him something akin to fame.

We made the traditional run to The Pig's Eye Saloon after the burial to, as Jamie Kennedy always said, "hoist one to the memory of the dearly departed."

Harry the Cat had indeed been a climber, a good one too, in the days of his youth. Clyde said "he would have climbed the Laurel this time too if it just hadn't been so blasted hot."

It was Mexican Joe who pointed out the obvious, "The cat man, wanted the world to know that he was still able to climb, and with the story in the paper his wish came true."

I guess we all hate the thought of getting old, or maybe we hate the thought that others are seeing us get old. We see ourselves as we were, and when others see us as we are now, that's when we want to climb the mountain, scale the building, run the race, to show them it's just not true, that like Harry The Cat, we will forever be, at least in our dreams, what we were in the days of our youth.

Chapter Six
Jamie and Alcoholics Anonymous

If drinking is interfering with your work, you're a heavy drinker.
If work is interfering with your drinking, you're an alcoholic.

I had worked for The International for several months doing mostly buildings, when Frank the Boss called me over one morning and asked how I was on plate glass.

I said, "I'm good on a truck route, that's all I did at the last company I worked for." Plate glass was a dream. Instead of climbing in and out of windows on the buildings all day, you had a truck route, in which you cleaned store fronts, plate glass, first floor windows. You worked fast and stayed on the ground. I liked that.

Frank said, "Jamie is short a man on the truck route today, he'll give you a try out."

Jamie Kennedy was a short stocky Irishman, with curly black hair, and a perpetual big wide toothy grin. He seemed to be smiling all the time, and was apparently really enjoying his life running the truck route.

We hit the street running at each stop, and he knew the shortest way between every job. There was no coffee break or 3.2 breaks when you worked the truck with Irish, as most of the crew called him. He started the morning on a run and didn't slow down until eleven. By then every job slip Frank had given us before we left the shop was done. We were out of work. Each job had been timed by Czech to give Frank a good day's work but still not force the crew to push too hard to get the jobs done on time. Irish went wide open from 7 to 11, and was then through for the day. I was amazed and said, "What do we do now; go back to the shop for more job slips."

"No," Irish said, "we're done, I plan it this way. We work hard, we get through by eleven, and head for the AA club. Frank knows where we are. As long as he doesn't get any complaints on the jobs we did this morning he's happy, and we spend the afternoon at the club."

Irish was a member and staunch supporter of Alcoholics Anonymous and would spend the afternoon playing cribbage with fellow AA members.

I headed for the upstairs reading room, where I could spread out my assignments from school and would spend 2 or 3 hours studying. That was a rare and much appreciated luxury since the radio engineering course at The American Institute of the Air was tough, and I wasn't that good at math.

Occasionally Frank the Boss would call during the afternoon and ask Irish if he could break away for an hour or two for a special job that was just called in. It worked well. Irish got to work on staying sober, and I got to work on my homework.

That first night he told Frank, "Herring Choker is good, he stayed with me all day and never left a streak, I checked his work over real good."

It was high praise coming from an old timer and I went home that night feeling good, and to class that night with all my homework done for the first time.

We stayed together as a team until I graduated from school and passed the audition for my first job as a radio announcer. Irish was as proud as I was the morning I told Frank the Boss I had passed all the FCC tests and was qualified to work as a radio announcer/engineer.

I had an official First Class Radio Telephone license issued by the Federal Communications Commission in Washington DC. I had passed an audition for an announcing job at a radio station and would soon be leaving the International to go to work as a radio announcer.

But that's getting ahead of the story.

One day shortly after I had begun working with him, I asked Jamie about his affiliation with the AA and how long had he been a member. He took a deep breath, swallowed hard and said, "Ain't nobody else on the crew asked me that and I don't know as how I want them to know."

I said, "fine with me, I don't have to know either." Irish took another deep breath, paused for a few seconds and said, "Well, I'll tell you. This is the way it was. I was a hard drinker. I would take one drink and then I just couldn't quit. I would go on a bender that would last for days, sometimes weeks at a time. One day, I came out of the haze in a court room. I was standing there in a fog. I didn't know what was happening. I was slipping in and out of this haze.

My stomach felt like it was turning end over end. My mouth was like dry cotton. I heard a voice saying, 'James Kennedy do you understand me? Do you understand what I am saying'? "The courtroom was nearly full. There were people all around. The sun coming through the windows was so bright it hurt to even open my eyes. It was hot. I couldn't get my breath. There were a couple of people holding on to my arms to keep me from falling over. I didn't know anyone."

Pausing for a moment he continued, "When the judge asked me again if I understood what was going on I mumbled something. He asked me again. 'Are you fully aware of what is happening here?' Well at that point I had to tell him that I didn't have the faintest idea what was happening and that every other time I went on a toot I would wake up in the holding tank at the county jail. I asked him why I was in court. The Judge said, 'James Kennedy, you took a man's life. You have been charged with manslaughter and today, through your attorney, you entered a guilty plea. This court is required to pass sentence on you. Mr. Kennedy, do you have anything you would like to say before I do so?'"

Irish said, "I don't really remember what happened next. My knees sort of went slack on me and I must have passed out. I couldn't believe what he had said. I had no memory of hurting anyone. I couldn't believe what I was hearing."

"James Kennedy," the Judge said, "I am sentencing you to the state prison at Stillwater, Minnesota for a term of not less than 7 and not more than 10 years."

"It was at just that moment," said Irish," that I became aware of a woman crying and saying no, no, no. I turned and saw my wife sitting in the first row. She was holding onto my son and crying as if she would never stop. That's the moment I quit drinking.

They let me see her for a few minutes before they marched me off to prison. I couldn't imagine that she would wait 10 years for a worthless drunken bum to get out of prison. At that moment I thought everything that mattered in my life was gone. 10 years? I wasn't worth waiting 5 minutes for. 10 years?

How could I expect her to wait and raise my son by herself?
But she did."

"I found out later I had been drunk out of my mind. That I killed a man in a brawl over a bottle. I killed him with my bare hands. I still can't believe I did that."

Irish raised his fists to the top of the truck's steering wheel, and just stared at them. A look of wonder and disgust in his eyes and on his face.

"They marched me through the gates at Stillwater State Prison and got me registered. The guard asked if I had any questions. I had only one. When does the AA Club meet?

My first meeting was that afternoon. I've been going ever since, and will until the day I die. I know now," said Irish, "that I can't stay off the booze by myself, but with the support of these friends at the club, I stay sober one day at a time. I need their help and that's why I need to work fast all morning, to get to the club as fast as I can."

Apparently Frank the Boss was the only one on the crew who knew about state prison and the manslaughter rap and that's the way it stayed.

Funny isn't it? A guy running away from the bottle gets hooked up with a bunch of people who spend their spare time chasing after one.

Irish seemed to need the association with the past to help him keep his future on track. The people around him could show him on a daily basis what he would be like if he was still on the sauce.

Irish and I had a pretty good summer, and we both benefited from the daily afternoon sessions at the St. Paul AA Club.

Chapter Seven - Chippewa Charlie
Until lions have their own historians,
tales of the hunt shall always glorify the hunters. African Proverb

Chippewa Charlie could clean a window faster than Czech or Blind Bob. And that was pretty fast. Evenings for Charlie were spent with Gorgeous George, Black Bill and others from the crew in what seemed to be a never ending tour of the just-below-the-loop hot spots.

Looking as if he had attended an all-night drinking party, which he probably had, Charlie would arrive at work just in time to hear Frank the Boss line out the jobs for the day. He would then throw a leather safety belt over his shoulders, pick up his job slips and bucket of tools and head for the nearest greasy spoon restaurant. There he would drink a breakfast of coffee and juice. A short time later he would be seen climbing out a window ten or fifteen floors above the sidewalks of downtown St. Paul, cleaning windows with great vigor. He was forever letting loose with what he apparently thought was an authentic Indian war hoop. It startled passersby if we were working in the downtown area but it got so the rest of us didn't pay too much attention.

One day while working on the old Fort Snelling Hospital, Charlie was on top of a forty foot extension ladder on a part of the lawn which sloped slightly downhill. While he was working, one leg of the ladder sank in to the soft soil of the lawn causing the top of the ladder to start sliding slowly sideways down the face of the building.

Now when you're forty feet up in the air on top of a ladder and it's slipping sideways you have a problem. Charlie let out a blood curdling scream and called out to the rest of the men who were working around the corner. No one paid any attention. They thought he was just doing one of those blasted war hoops again. It wasn't until after the third or fourth scream that someone poked his head around the corner to shout at him and found Charlie tipping sideways at a terrible angle, hanging on to a large brick protruding from the bottom of a window. They grabbed his ladder and got him straightened out.

A few minutes later he walked off the job and into a 3.2 beer joint down the street. We didn't see him for a couple of days.

It was an informal sort of thing, accepted as a part of life that guys disappeared occasionally. Sometimes with some Muscatel wine to drink their way into forgetfulness. Sometimes, when the DT's hit them hard, they would end up at the state hospital at Willmar to take the cure, dry out and get three hots and a cot until they were able to stand up straight again. Occasionally it would be to try and drink a couple of taverns dry while they used up a windfall like an income tax return check. Frank would just shake his head and wait for their return.

Monday morning bull sessions were always a little quieter than those later in the week. Many of the crew members were coming off their weekend binge. They would look like they had spent the night in a dumpster. Red watery eyes, puffy faces and bad dispositions. Some were openly hostile to anyone laughing or making otherwise loud noises. A sure fire topic was the latest fad for taking care of a hangover. Tomato juice, ice cubes on the back of the neck, aspirin in half a coke. Someone always had a new miracle cure that would take away the ravages of a long weekend filled with booze, smoke, and little sleep. The hangover cures never seemed to work. One of the nondrinkers was sure to ask, "why do you do it when each weekend ends up the same way?"

The non-drinker couldn't understand of course that the binge drinking wasn't something you just turned off by yourself. The exceptions were men like Jamie Kennedy who had bottomed out. Hit bottom and through the support of his wife and the people in AA who had gone through the same thing, was able to face the faceless beast and overcome it.

Like most of those who succeeded, Jamie had found a new faith in God. A spiritual rebirth was the ultimate solution to the Monday morning hangover problem.

A regular Monday morning routine found Jamie arriving a little early, so he could be there when Chippewa Charlie arrived. Charlie was a quiet one. He would arrive looking pasty faced and red eyed and sit quietly through the bull session while Frank the Boss lined out the day's work.

Throughout the session Charlie would sit to one side, eyes downcast, saying nothing.

Jamie would sit down beside him, and begin a quiet conversation, mostly one way, with little response from Charlie.

One morning, after we started our run for the day I asked Jamie what was the deal with Charlie. Why did he get drunk every weekend and blow his meager wages on the booze.

Jamie said, "There is never a simple answer. Alcoholics don't need a reason for their actions. Their bodies react to the disease of alcoholism and they just react to the booze and most probably have no idea why they do what they do."

When I told Jamie I thought the AA club where we spent our afternoons seemed to really help and maybe he should get Charlie to spend some time there.

He smiled and said, "You just don't understand the program. The club we go to each day is just a place where AA members can get together for some comradeship in a place where no booze is served. But the meeting place is not the AA club. Alcoholics Anonymous is in our minds. It's in our service to those who drink and don't understand. It's a spiritual feeling that comes from following the twelve steps. It's belief in a supreme being. It's admitting that we are not able to help ourselves. AA is what we believe and what we do, not where we go to be with friends. Does that make sense?"

I said, "I thought the building was Alcoholics Anonymous but it's really the feeling men have when they have beaten booze and are trying to help others?"

"You see," Jamie said, "Most of us couldn't stay off the booze if we didn't share the story. It's the sharing that keeps us sober and keeps us trying. We're all one drink away from being back on the sauce again but we know we can beat it if we keep sharing."

"Well how about Charlie, I see you visiting with him every Monday morning, but he doesn't stop, isn't there anything AA can do for him?"

"No," he said, "AA can't do anything for him. He has to do it for himself. All we can do is be there for him when he finally hits bottom. When he finally admits he can't stop by himself, and when something happens that makes him want to reach out for help, that's when we need to be there for him, that's when we can help."

He said, "You can't really understand since you've never felt the pain of being completely alone, hopeless, and helpless.

He ended up shaking his head and with his usual grin, said, "The only thing you teetotalers need to understand is that it works. It really works."

A few days later, as the crew was getting ready to leave the bull session and head out for the day's runs one of the old timers turned to Charlie and said, "C'mon Geronimo, let's get a move on, we've got a day's work to do."

Charlie looked up with fire in his eyes. In an angry voice he said, "My name is Charlie. My name is not Geronimo, don't call me Geronimo!"

It was such an unusual outburst from the usually taciturn Indian that when we were all checked in that night I sat down beside him and asked why he had gotten so upset when the old guy called him Geronimo.

"He didn't mean anything by it, he was just using a nick name like they use on all of us."

Charlie looked at the floor and in a voice almost a whisper said, "Geronimo was a great leader of his people. I am a great nothing. They shouldn't call a great nothing by the name of a great leader."

With that he walked out of the shop and didn't come back to work for the rest of the week.

Chippewa Charlie saw Geronimo as a great leader! I guess I had never thought a lot about Geronimo. If and when I had I'm sure it was a vision of the cavalry pursuing rampaging Indians across the badlands of the west as they were depicted in the western movies.

My friend Charlie's picture of Geronimo was of a great leader who led his outgunned-out-manned forces against the white race which was invading his homeland. An alien race, spreading across their homeland, destroying everything the Indian people valued, as they went. The high mucky mucks who write the history books with black ink on white paper or print the films in Hollywood couldn't see Geronimo as a great leader who was writing his peoples history in his blood.

Charlie saw the real history of the country being written in the blood of his people, as the man he saw as a great leader, led his warrior forces into battle.

Next morning I asked Jamie about that. "Is that why he drinks? Because he thinks he is a nothing, a nobody?"

"Well," said Jamie, "We all drink for different reasons.

That's as good a reason as any." He didn't say any more, and was unusually quiet the rest of the morning.

Each day soon after we arrived at the AA building on Kellogg Boulevard Jamie would head for the phone and would soon be talking to his wife. This was a routine that never varied from day to day. His AA friends kidded him about reporting in to "the ball and chain," before he could get down to the serious business of their daily cribbage game.

But that wasn't it, and I could see it.

On the morning call to his wife; his voice seemed to take on a different, softer tone. It was like awe, or reverence. It was obvious this was a very important person in his life. She was a person who had stayed with him when he hit bottom, who had supported him during his years in prison, and who was still there, loving him, when he stepped through the prison gates and walked back into her life a free man.

Or as he put it, "Free from the iron bars of prison but on lifetime parole from the bottle. Once you're hooked on booze," he said, "you're never free again, only on parole."

It was almost as if he expected no answer when he called his wife and was filled with wonder all over again when she answered the phone and he knew she was still there for him.

Although tears never showed in his eyes, you could almost hear them in his voice. They would talk for a moment and she would know he had made it through another morning. He was with the friends who would help him through the afternoon. He was like that as he sat down beside Chippewa Charlie on Monday mornings too. He would occasionally say a few words, quietly, softly, and would always give him a little pat on the back or shoulder as he got up to leave the shop for the morning run. As if to say, "I've been there man, I know your feelings, and I understand, but I can't give you any help until you ask for it."

It was getting on toward fall the morning we ran into Charlie while out on our route. He was working a second story ladder job next to the store where we were cleaning the first floor plate glass windows.

Jamie shouted a greeting as we climbed out of the truck, but before Charlie could answer, there was a commotion in the doorway of the store.

A large man was in the process of throwing a small boy out of the store and was shouting at the top of his lungs.

"Get out and stay out you thievin' Indian," he stormed, and added a hard kick at the youngster's legs for good measure. The force of the kick sent the Indian youth slamming headlong into the side of our truck. He bounced off the fender and fell into the gutter.

Jamie stepped over to help the boy up while Charlie, with one long step, faced the angry store owner and said, "He's just a boy, you kicked him, and he's just a boy."

"Yeah, he's just a kid but he'll grow up to be a big no account red skin like you," shouted the still angry store owner.

It was the last thing we heard from him.

Charlie's fist seemed to start at his ankles. It rose quickly to the height of the store owner's chin. The man's head snapped backward, and the angry light in his eyes faded away.

From the look in Charlie's eyes, it was apparent that with that one swing, all the hurt from all those years of being called Indian, Red Skin and Geronimo was being blown away. He hadn't held anything back. The angry store owner got it all.

With that one mighty blow to the chin Charlie lifted the businessman clear off his feet and sent him flying through the plate glass window.

As the heavy glass shattered, blood from the cuts flowed freely. People started running from the back of the store. Pedestrians backed away. A siren could be heard echoing off the walls of the buildings.

Jamie said, "C'mon Charlie, you better get outta here."

"No," Charlie said, "The police will be here soon, and I'll be here too."

The charges were heavy. Charlie, unable to make bail, stayed in jail until his day in court arrived. Frank the Boss, Jamie, Czech and Clyde went over to the courthouse to speak for Charlie and it helped Charlie's cause when Frank agreed to pay the damages. The store owner wasn't hurt bad, and Frank took care of his wounded pride by offering to have his crew clean the windows on his store for an entire year at no charge.

Frank, Charlie, and his coworkers left the courthouse and crossed Kellogg Boulevard together.

As they headed for the company trucks in the city parking lot across the street, Charlie quietly asked Jamie if he could show him around Alcoholics Anonymous.

He had hit bottom.

The stint in jail and the court appearance made this a turning point.

With Jamie's help he was about to embark on his climb up and off the skid and out of the clutch of alcohol.

It was like Jamie said, "We can't make them come, we can only be here for them when they're ready. And it's not all just for them; it's for those of us who are sober too. Sharing the program is the only way we can make it work for us. We can't stay sober if we don't share all the feelings we've gone through with those who are going through it now. It's when they realize we're talking their language they understand we really do know down deep how they are feeling. That's when the light goes on and for the first time they can really hear what we're saying."

It was a new Charlie coming in on Monday mornings. A sober man who seemed to grow more thoughtful and quiet with each passing week.

Only Jamie and those who attended the regular AA meetings ever heard Charlie's whole story, and of course that was the one part of the program that is never shared with anyone but those who attend the meetings.

Chapter Eight - Charlie and the Kid

We worry about what a child will become tomorrow,
yet we forget that he is someone today. Stacia Tauscher

On a Monday morning in late November Charlie arrived at the shop with a bruise covering most of one cheek. In the old days this wouldn't have been unusual but he didn't look as if he had fallen off the wagon.
He just looked mighty tender and sore.

Charlie was reluctant to explain the bruise until Frank, said, "C'mon Charlie, fill us in, what does the other guy look like?" He added with a chuckle, "Will we have to go to court for you?"

"No boss, it's nothin' like that. It's hockey, I coach the kid's hockey team and got on the wrong end of a slap shot."

At that the room was fairly buzzing. The Indian? Chippewa Charlie coaching hockey? The drunken Indian from the Blue Lake Reservation coaching kids?

"It was the kid," Charlie said, in answer to the puzzled looks from other members of the crew. "The kid that got kicked out of the store for stealing and got me thrown in to the cross bar hotel for busting the store owner. I tracked him down and found out he and the other kids were playing ice hockey with brooms and a cover from an old kettle.

I played hockey back on the Res and I'm trying to get the kids off the street and into a park board hockey league."

Charlie had indeed played ice hockey and as we learned later had led his ill-equipped teen-aged team from the Blue Lake Reservation in Northern Minnesota all the way to the state tournament. It was during the tournament he got kicked off the squad for drinking between periods of a playoff game.

The big Indian as a teen age center had led his front line into the fray all over Northern Minnesota. Despite the Indian team's lack of equipment and financial support they had played the perennial powerhouse Duluth Central, the Rangers from the little town of Mountain Iron and several of the other Iron Range High School teams. They played'em to a standstill and won a berth in the state hockey tournament.

No one knew this at the time of course, since Charlie just didn't talk about his past life.

The story of Chippewa Charlie's prowess on the ice came to light much later. A reporter heard about his efforts to give the kids from the tenement's a chance to play in an organized park board league and did a full page feature on them.

But that's getting ahead of the story.

The morning the crew learned about his efforts, he was besieged with questions about the kids, his knowledge of hockey, and his ability to put together a team.

It was Czech who brought the questions into focus.

"How many kids you got and what kind of equipment do you need?" he asked Charlie.

Charlie said, "we have about twenty five kids if they all come out. Some don't come all the time. They don't have the clothes to keep warm if it's real cold. They would probably come if we could get the shin guards, pads and sweat shirts they need. Most of them don't even have decent hockey skates, so we have a long way to go. If any of you have any ideas on where we could get money for equipment, let me know."

It was an unlikely group to ask. What did the skinners of the International know about hockey, kids, or fund raising?

Orbit slid over to Czech and said, "Meet me at the Pig's Eye before you start your run, I have an idea to help Charlie."

A short time later not only were Clyde and Czech at the Pig's Eye, but the rest of the crew too. Waiting for Orbit and his idea.

"Here's the deal." said Orbit, "You know I go to night school over at the University. A guy in my Wednesday night class is a trainer with the Gopher hockey team. I could talk to him about these kids but I don't know what to ask him for."

"Skates and shin guards," said Clyde, "They can play without the rest of the pads but they have to have hard toe hockey skates and shin guards. And they have to have goalie pads so some hot shot doesn't kill the kid in the net with a slap shot from the blue line."

"Where did you learn about hockey Clyde?" asked Czech.

"I live near East Park and watch the kids play on Saturday.

They really go at it. Unless Charlie's kids get the right pads there'll be a real Indian massacre the first time they play one of these regular teams."

"All right Orbit," said Czech, "does that help?

We need skates for twenty five kids, and shin guards, as well as the other pads, and sticks. Don't forget hockey sticks. If your friend the trainer has any pull, get him to throw in the sticks."

We never did find out what Orbit told his classmate that Wednesday night, but the trainer went to the coaches of the Gopher hockey teams. He told them about this young Indian guy who was trying to help the poor kids stay off the streets by getting them into a hockey league.

Since the class was on family and community relations with an emphasis on minorities and juvenile delinquency it was a natural. Most of the class asked if they could get involved. They could use the program for a class project from a research angle. Several volunteered to join the trainer in his attempts to get cast off equipment from the U of M squad.

After several meetings the Gopher team members and athletic department officials, agreed to informally adopt Charlie's kids and began gathering up old equipment. Early the following Saturday morning as Charlie and his kids were trying to practice with their makeshift gear a Gopher team bus pulled up at the small neighborhood ice rink.

The youthful members of the would-be hockey team fell silent as first one and then another saw the bus with the University of Minnesota Golden Gopher Hockey emblems on the side.

As the university players began stepping off the bus carrying bags full of equipment the usually exuberant kids were completely silent.

The assistant coach walked over to Charlie and said, "One of the guys you work with told us you were starting a kid's hockey team and that you don't have enough equipment. We'd like to help if it's okay with you."

The big Indian couldn't say a word. His mouth seemed to open a couple of times but nothing came out. He could do nothing but stare at this answer to a hockey team's prayer.

"Charlie? Charlie Blackdeer, is that you? It is you isn't it? We all wondered what happened to you after you left the team during the tournament. The officials said you violated tournament rules and they asked you to leave. Where you been man? Where you been?"

"Every goalie in the state was glad you were off the ice, you had the fastest slap shot around. I can't believe this, why didn't you call us man, we would have come any time. You shoulda called us Charlie."

Charlie, recognized by someone from his past life just shook his head and looked down at the ice, "I couldn't John," he said. "I just couldn't face anyone after I got drunk and ruined my team's chances at state. I just couldn't face anyone and I don't know that I can now either."

"All right," said the coach, "you guys wanna hold a reunion get off the ice we wanna fit these kids with some of our old skates and pads. Line up by the warm up bench you guys, short kids on the left, tall on the right. Move it, move it, c'mon, we wanna get these pads on so we can play a little hockey before the sun goes down, let's go, let's go."

And with that the Gopher team members began lining the teen agers up by the bench and started fitting them with the skates, shin guards and pads from the bags of used equipment they brought with them.

It could have been Christmas, birthdays and all the other holidays rolled into one from the looks on the faces of Charlie's kids. This was a day like none they had ever known. For a group of kids living just off the skid row in those run down old apartments and used to being looked down on and pushed or kicked out of the way of regular people this was something else. It seemed like all the high mucky mucks in the city had converged on their poor side of town and wanted to help make the hurt of being poor go away.

With coaching assistance from the Gopher hockey squad and equipment that made them feel like pros Charlie and his kids had taken a big step toward getting enough credibility to be accepted into the city Park Board League.

The following Monday morning Charlie thanked the crew, especially Orbit for all of their help in bringing his kids this bonanza of equipment. The big man was a little shaken yet and seemed to be having a hard time believing their good fortune.

"What else does your team need Charlie?" asked Frank.
"Well there's some kind of an insurance policy we have to have before they'll let us play in the park board league. Charlie replied.

"The kids can play without them, but it would be nice to have team sweat shirts with a name on them. We'll have to try and find something we can do to raise money; the kids are all willing to work."

"How about transportation to the games, do you have a way to haul those kids around?"

"No, we thought we might get parents but most of them don't own a car. They have trouble just getting rent, heat, and food most of the time."

"Tell you what, Charlie, since most of the games are on Saturday, if you come up with money for your insurance and a couple of drivers, you can take a couple of company trucks. But you make sure those kids know that they have to sit down if you haul them around in the back. We don't want anyone hurt."

Once again Charlie looked stunned. The offers of help for his kids seemed to keep on coming. After so many years of feeling that everybody in St. Paul looked down on the reservation refugees, to find out that many people actually seemed to care was almost too much to comprehend.

It was the ex-window cleaner, Preacher Roy, who solved the sweat shirt problem for Charlie and his kids.

The Skid Row Mission he had helped found to serve the women who lived on the skid and worked the street corners as their profession had started a vocational training program. A commercial sewing business. They produced denim jackets, and vests which were sold in outlets all over the cities.

When Preacher heard about Charlie's kids he met with the group of women and they started working on sweat shirts. They not only sewed the shirts in several sizes, they also cut out large block letters and put a name on the back of each garment.

Preacher named the team. When the jerseys were brought out Saturday morning during the weekend practice they not only brought cheers from the kids but a round of applause from the university players who were on hand to help coach, and from parents and other spectators who came to watch the practice sessions.

The name, in big letters on the back of each player's sweatshirt was, The International Americans.

Everyone there had to admit the name was right.

The International, because of all the help from Frank and the members of his crew, Americans because this group of players, mostly from the Blue Lake Indian Reservation were really "Americans".

It looked like the International Americans hockey team was on its way, and it looked like Charlie had found his answer too.

Through Jamie and the AA club he had discovered a faith in a higher power and the knowledge that if he was to win the battle with booze, it was going to be through his efforts to help others win their battles too.

Ironic isn't it? You think you're fighting the world all by yourself, and then someone hears about the battle and you find that all the high mucky mucks will pitch in and help too, if you just give them a chance.

Charlie's Americans, as the team was usually called, may have lacked playing finesse in the usual sense, but from the youngest to the oldest they brought a fire and passion to the game that was all too often missing.

As Charlie worked his way through his illness and the period of sobriety got longer and longer, his work with his hockey team became an increasingly important part of his life and he became increasingly important in the lives of the young people he worked with.

The youth most responsible for his being there was the kid who was thrown out of the store and kicked by the owner the day Charlie got thrown in jail. After his jail time Charlie spent weeks walking the streets and checking the usual haunts for the slum kids, before finding him on the improvised hockey rink, behind a warehouse.

His name was Cary Crazy Wolf, and he lived with his mother and several brothers and sisters in an apartment house a few blocks off the lower loop, in the seamy warehouse district.

The rent was cheap and so were the landlords who owned blocks of ancient buildings converted to apartments. The neighborhood was filled with Indians from the Northern Minnesota Reservations, Mexicans, legal or otherwise and several other ethnic groups struggling to find a way of life in a community populated by people of northern European heritage. Most of these latter were at least one generation removed from their immigrant ancestors and had forgotten or perhaps never even knew the feeling of being alone in an alien land. Charlie's kids knew the feeling. They lived it every day.

Cary Crazy Wolf, or El Lobo Loco as the Mexican kids called him, had been in other scrapes with the law besides the one which got Charlie in trouble. Despite being small for his age, he carried an air of bravado that helped him get by in a world of big kids and tough neighborhoods.

It was Crazy Wolf that Charlie had sought out and Crazy Wolf who Charlie wanted to help with the hockey team.

The kid couldn't really skate. He minced his way across the ice on the sides of his feet with his weak ankles bending over at a sharp angle.

He made up for lack of skill with an unyielding determination and an ever present grin, even though he spent much of his time on the bench waiting for the coach to call his name.

As the Americans worked their way through their first season of park board hockey, they managed, with the help of the university hockey team coaches to win more than they lost. They stayed in contention when everyone around them thought they would fall from the standings. Seemingly down for the count, they would come through with the clutch goal and eke out yet another win.

This despite Charlie's insistence that every member of the team from the best players to the worst get playing time in every game. If you practice you play was his motto.

That playing time included El Lobo Loco, who may not have scored in his position as a defense man, but who fought furiously for the puck if it came anywhere near him.

He would, with the slightest provocation, throw off his heavy gloves and with fists flailing wildly wade into any player who knowingly or unknowingly offended him, just as he had seen the pros do it.

After the season ending playoffs in February, the two top teams in the Twin Cities would receive a treat that was talked about by every player in the entire league at every practice.

The Twin City Park Board League championship game would be played between the periods of a regular season game of the professional hockey team, the Minneapolis Millers.

Here was a thrill that every park board league hockey player in the cities yearned for. To play on the same ice as the pros like Glen Sonmor or John Mariucci.

To play the championship game under the vast roof of the old arena where the top hockey players of the nation played. That was the dream.

Some even dared hope that Gordie Howe would lead his fabled Detroit Red Wings against the Millers the night the league championship would be decided. Here was a reward worthy of long hours of practice, a goal to be burned into the minds of every youth hockey player in the cities. It was the subject of lengthy discussions by members of the International Americans as well. No one dared even hope that in their first year they could reach this pinnacle of youth hockey achievement, yet their dream continued to hang by a thread.

Each time it appeared their hopes would be dashed, a lucky break, an extra shot on goal, a great save by a goalie, some event would take place to preserve their standing in the league.

And so it was that the newest team in the Twin City Park Board Hockey League, with help from Preacher's ex prostitutes, assistance from the Golden Gopher hockey team, and with the coaching of Chippewa Charlie, recovering alcoholic, ended the season number one in St. Paul. The crucial game came, pitting them against the team that was number one in the Minneapolis standings, the powerful Robbinsville Rangers.

The team from the northwest corner of the cities was well equipped with corporate sponsors who provided top-of-the-line equipment. Their community had the wherewithal to provide an indoor ice rink and practice facility.

The Rangers were big, strong and fast, and this game would be played on the ice of the Arena, between the periods of the professional hockey game. The winner would be the new Twin City Champion.

The game, was scoreless through the first and second periods, as the Americans' goalie made save after save and the Rangers made one front line power sweep after another, skating through the Americans' defensive line, seemingly at will. As the final minutes of the third period ticked away the game appeared to be headed for a sudden death overtime which would be played after the conclusion of the professional game.

With only a couple of minutes left in the final period, Charlie called out, "Crazy Wolf, get in there."

The call brought stunned looks from the kids teammates, as well as the university hockey players who attended as many International American games as possible.

Crazy Wolf? The least talented player on the team! On the ice to play defense against some of the biggest strongest players in the league? And with only a few minutes to go in the championship game?

They all knew Charlie felt strongly that every player from the best to the worst, had to have playing time in every game.
He insisted, if they practiced, they played.

But this was the championship game itself. These final minutes on the professional arena ice could determine the Twin City champions.

Crazy Wolf didn't even wait for the opening of the gate, but went over the boards instead, and more running than skating sped across the ice toward the blue line where what could be the final face off of the game was about to take place.

A groan went up from some of the American fans as they saw the smallest least talented member of the team cross the ice but it was quickly silenced by a dark look from the coach as he turned toward those making the sound.

The sticks of the players in the circle raised to lightly touch each other once, twice, and a third time as the puck dropped from the official's hand toward that tiny spot on the ice where it would land. The fraction of a second it took the puck to fall from the outstretched hand of the official to the hockey sticks waiting to slam it toward a waiting team mate seemed to last forever. For those watching from behind the boards it seemed to be falling in slow motion. It didn't seem forever to the Americans who won the face off as a stick only a split second faster than that of the Rangers, sent the puck swiftly across the ice toward the blue line in front of the Rangers goal. Crazy Wolf was off like a shot as were two Ranger defense men. Short, fast steps carried the diminutive player across the ice, toward the fast moving puck. The crowd roared and players from both teams rose from the benches and crowded the sideboards of the rink.

For Charlie, the first year coach, the has been high school hockey star of the Iron Range, the action was frozen into a collage, a series of snapshot images.

Crazy Wolf caught up with the puck a split second before the two much larger defenders. He swung his stick as if it were a driver being used for a tee shot on a golf course, not a hockey stick being used for a slap shot on goal in the final seconds of the championship game.

The stick striking the puck at an angle sent it upward, between the outstretched sticks of the Ranger defense men who arrived at the same spot a split second later.

The puck lifted, and then turned over on its side, taking two long bounces as it sped toward the goalie. Had it been a good shot, the slap shot of one of the better players; it would have lifted a short distance off the ice and then sped like an arrow toward the net and the waiting glove of the goalie. But it was not a good shot; it didn't fly through the air toward the goal. It bounced, skittering across the ice it slammed into the goalie's skate blade and rolled between his legs into the net.

The red light went on! The goal was made. The game was won. The championship was theirs.

The International Americans were The Twin City Champions.

For the first time all night the arena was dead silent.

Not a sound from a crowd that had cheered and shouted at the slightest movement.

All eyes turned from the net to the spot from whence the winning shot had been made. But where was Crazy Wolf?

Having made the impossible shot his skates had flown from beneath him sending him flying full speed into the legs, feet and skates of the defenders who were bowled over by the force of Crazy Wolf's fall.

As the Ranger Defense men untangled themselves and stood up, they were alone on their feet. The kid didn't move.

A spot of blood on the forehead showed where his head had struck the skate blade of one of the defenders.

A gasp went up from the Americans' bench and his team mates flew over the boards to go after the Robbinsville players who had brought harm to their teammate.

The largest of the Rangers bent down, picked Crazy Wolf up from the ice and headed toward the American bench.

"We didn't do anything, we didn't do anything," he repeated several times as the swarm of Indian players closed in.

The crowd remained silent as the still quiet Crazy Wolf was handed over to Charlie who had joined his team on the ice.

As Charlie carried him toward the bench, the kid's eyes opened. Lifting his head he asked in a small, quiet voice, "Did we score coach? Did we score?"

As Charlie called out to teammates and supporters, "He's okay, he's okay," a roar went up from the crowd behind the Americans bench.

"Lobo Loco, Lobo Loco, Lobo Loco," it was a chant that began slowly then became louder and faster.

"Lobo Loco, Lobo Loco," it grew in volume as more and more voices joined in the cheer to honor the diminutive hero.

A few scattered boos from some of the die-hard Ranger fans were quickly silenced when the Robbinsville team captain vaulted over the side of the boards and with raised hands began shouting in unison with the International Americans fans, the chant, "Lobo Loco, Lobo Loco."

Without knowing what the name meant, knowing only that it was being directed toward the tiny tornado who had so recently sped across the ice to make his game winning shot, the crowd joined in the chant until the steel girders in the roof reverberated with the intensity and volume.

As the chant continued a Minneapolis Miller skated swiftly across the ice and took the now wide awake Crazy Wolf from Charlie's arms and lifting him to his shoulders the professional hockey player began a slow parade lap around the rink.

With the chant Lobo Loco ringing in his ears and seated high above the ice on the shoulders of the professional hockey player Crazy Wolf was experiencing every kid's dream.

And so were his team members who moved in behind Crazy Wolf and his new found guardian and did still another parade lap while professional hockey players from both of the teams playing that evening moved out behind them filling the ice rink with a colorful, parade of skaters.

Telling about it now it sounds like a fairy tale, but that's the way it was.

I do believe that occasionally life does compensate those who have been kicked around or pushed back and held down, by giving them that special moment they will cherish in their heart. That golden moment of victory that will lie there in the far back recesses of the mind, until at some point, when they've again been knocked down, pushed aside, and trampled on, at that moment when they need the boost most of all, then will that bright, golden moment of victory come quickly forward to remind them of the past and it's shining moments. The golden moment will come again if you just hang in there and keep on trying.

When the high mucky mucks lay down the rules that will hold you back, and keep you looking down at the dirty, garbage strewn sidewalk as you walk down their streets, this moment of victory will return again and again to help get your chin up, to help you look them in the eye as you pass, and will give you the inner strength to take the risk of trying again.

It is that moment of victory that will live forever in their minds as they face the uncertainties of an uncertain life.

But Charlie, Jamie Kennedy and thousands of others trying to recover from the illness of alcoholism know that each moment they stay sober is their victory. Each hour they don't take that drink, each morning they awake with clear eyes and a clear mind is a victory.

And they know, too, that without each of those small victories they are only one drink away from being back on the sauce and back on the skid.

Chippewa Charlie had come full circle. From high school hockey star on Minnesota's Iron Range, to big city skid row drunk. With help from Jamie Kennedy and other AA Club members and with what he called an assist from the Great Spirit he made his move back into the real world.

It was a tough education. In the 50's being a reservation Indian in the big cities presented plenty of problems by itself. The move back into the real world from the cities skid row was a giant step. A step that took more courage than most of the rest of us will ever know or will ever need to know for the things we do.

For Charlie it was part of his rehabilitation. As the guys in AA said, "You can't make it yourself unless you pass it on to someone else."
Charlie, by helping his teen age Indian protégé's stay off the street and off the sauce that had gotten him in so much trouble was indeed, giving it back.

Charlie knew the real fight, the booze that took him down when he was a kid on the Iron Range, was waiting to take him down again.

He knew, and Jamie Kennedy knew, that his real fight would never end, that the temptation to have "just one drink" would always be there. But they also knew that a group of friends was going to be there too, and that sometimes, if you slipped on your way out of the pit, and had to start over, there would be helping hands to help you get back on your feet.

For Charlie, knowing he was not alone, and knowing he had the strength of his new found faith in a higher power would help put him back on the wagon again.

And it was obvious during the Saturday morning practice that as far as Charlie's kids were concerned, he was no longer "the great nothing" he had called himself that far off day during the afternoon bull session at the International Window Cleaning Company of the Twin Cities.

He stood tall in their eyes. To the kids and their parents he was like the legendary Geronimo, a great leader of his people.

Chapter Nine - Risks Vs. Rewards

To dare is to lose one's footing momentarily.
To not dare is to lose oneself. Soren Kierkegaard

The President was asked to comment on the risk he was taking by bringing the Arab and Jewish governments together at Camp David to try and work out a peace plan. He talked at length about the need to solve the problems of the Arab world and the rewards that would be the worlds if a peace plan were finalized. How they had tried to measure the risks and balance them with the expected rewards.

Sometimes people have different ideas about the rewards for success and penalties for failure.

Two people can look at the same thing and see it through different eyes, through different backgrounds and come up with different ideas about value. Sometimes we do things out of pride, and sometimes because you just have to do what you have to do.

That's the way it was when Gorgeous George made me a bet on how many chin ups I could do. It started innocently enough. One morning in the bull session he called over to me, "Hey Herring choker, I'll bet you ten bucks you can't do ten chin ups."

Everyone sort of looked up surprised like. Ten chin ups? That was nothing; everyone on the crew could handle that.

"What's the catch, George, what have you got up your sleeve this time?" I asked.

We all knew George, he only bet on sure things, and he was always looking for a way to get somebody.

He had grown up on the streets and had a mean streak, not like most of the guys who were tough but never tried to take advantage of each other, and were ready to help whenever someone needed a hand.

Not George. He was always ready to put one over on somebody as if it built him up or made him feel better about himself to beat someone.

Well George made the offer and said, "No catch, Herring Choker, just ten chin ups. Afraid you can't do that many?"

Without a second thought, I said, "You're on, I can do ten chin ups without even breathing hard, get your ten spot out and let's do it right here and now."

But George replied in a voice loud enough for everyone to hear, "It's getting late and since we're both going to be working "The Mutch," we can do it there and I'll choose the place.

The Mutch was the Minnesota Mutual Insurance Building.

He did a little snickering as he whispered to a couple of the others and from the looks on their faces I knew this would be no regular contest.

It was only after we got to the job site that he let me in on what he had in mind. We had barely gotten in the door when he said, "C'mon, let's see if you can do your ten chin ups and win a ten spot the easy way."

He headed for the elevator and punched up the eleventh floor. When we arrived there we didn't head for a storage room or the janitor's closet where we could find a pipe near the ceiling to do the chin ups from. Instead, George led the way to the exit and out on to the fire escape.

"There it is," he said, "there's the bar you can do your chin ups from, or would you rather just pay me my ten bucks now?"

From the look in his eyes as he pointed out the steel bar that braced the two sections of fire escape together I could see he thought it was a done deal.

Looking over the railing, it was eleven stories straight down to the sidewalk. There was nothing below the steel fire escape.

It was a mean trick. The kind of thing you could expect from Gorgeous George. The look on his face plainly said I'm smart and you're a fool and that's why you're gonna fork over ten of your hard earned dollars.

We both knew I could do ten chin ups without even breaking a sweat. When you jumped a couple of feet off the floor and grabbed the chin up bar the reward was plain. The penalty for failure minimal. If you slipped you only fell a couple of feet. But here, with the chin up bar being the steel brace between two sections of fire escape eleven floors above the street, the penalty for failure had gone up considerably. The reward for winning seemed to have diminished greatly in value.

As I looked down at the cars and trucks they looked pretty small. People looked even smaller as they walked by on the sidewalk unaware of the drama that was being played out eleven floors above them on the side of the old building.

I took a long look at the sidewalk below and at the steel bar inches away on the other side of the railing. I looked at George who had a smirk on his face that plainly said, "I got ya, fork over the ten spot."

That's when I lifted my leg over the top of the railing.

Oh I know it was foolish. But I knew I could do ten chin ups under more normal circumstances. There was no reason why I couldn't do them eleven floors up in the air. Sure the penalty for failure was higher but as I looked at George and saw the enjoyment he was getting out of the predicament he had put me in I knew there was only one thing I could do.

Office workers curious about the open fire escape door and the window cleaner who was climbing over the fire escape railing without a safety belt, began peering out of windows along the side of the building. Apparently the grapevine was spreading the news that there was a bet on.

I remember hearing a voice saying "Don't do it, don't do it," and another saying "go ahead, you can make it."

I broke out in a light sweat and had to rub my hands on my pants to dry them off. As I straddled the steel railing I took several deep breaths and looked, first down at the sidewalk eleven floors below, and then up at the steel railing jutting out from the side of the building.

George sounding a little worried said, "You crazy? You can't do this. C'mon pay me the ten bucks and let's get to work."

The rest of it was like a blur. Like a slow motion movie. I reached out for the steel bar. My throat got dry. I got a sharp pain in my groin and my breathing was rapid and shallow. I heard a loud buzzing noise in my ears. The voices of onlookers seemed to become fainter as I reached out and grabbed the bar with both hands. With a defiant look at George I swung loose from the railing and edged out hand over hand a couple of feet further away from the fire escape platform.

"Start counting, George," I gasped as I began the first lift, "Start counting."

It was over in a matter of minutes. It really doesn't take long to do ten chin ups. As spectators picked up the count I realized a crowd had gathered at windows all along the side of the building. They were chanting "three, four, five, six."

You could hear the volume go up with each chin up. "Seven, eight, nine, ten," and then a loud voice shouted "What in heaven's name is going on out here? Get your blankety blank back on this platform and you do it now!"

It was the Building Super attracted by the crowd and the chant. He was taking charge of his building.

With the last chin up completed I swung hand over hand ever so slowly back toward the fire escape.

A cheer went up from the crowd which by now had extended to a couple of other floors of the building as well.

As I swung over the railing with a triumphant look at Gorgeous George I was collared by the Super who literally dragged me inside and down the hall to his office.

"Ten bucks George, ten bucks," I called back down the hall, "You can pay me tonight back in the shop after the whole crew is in."

"Well," said the Super, "you won the bet, but it's gonna cost you."

He called Frank the Boss and explained in no uncertain terms what had happened. He ordered Frank to come over immediately to discipline the window cleaners who had caused the disruption in the operation of his building.

"That really was a fool thing to do," he said, as we waited for Frank. "What on earth made you take a chance like that?"

I really couldn't answer. It wasn't the ten bucks.

How do you explain to someone that it was the look in George's eye and the smirk on his face. That it was like the gunslinger baiting the sheriff in the old time western movie. It was just time to call him out. To say "George, this was a rotten trick, and I'm not going to let you get away with it."

I couldn't really say anything like that to the Super or to Frank when he came either.

All I could do was let them think I was crazy enough to take a dare. But Frank knew. He had heard the bet being made in the bull session that morning. He knew George, and he knew me. Without my saying it, he knew. That didn't help though when the Super insisted I be punished for my transgression and Frank suspended me for a day to make it look good.

I lost a day's wages with the suspension. But I won the bet and George had to pay off in front of the entire crew.

Sometimes the reward and penalty thing gets all out of focus. You have to look past what seems to make good sense at the moment and just do what you gotta do. That's what the president was doing at Camp David. It was a risk. But the rewards could be great.

George didn't rag on anybody for quite a while after that. A couple of times he actually bought coffee when we were out on a job together. It was almost like he had a new respect for me because I had called his bluff and backed him down.

I say almost because it wasn't long before he was the same old George. Ready to needle someone in the bull session or try to get them to do the outside on all the jobs on a cold day. He never did change much but he laid off me for quite a while. And I'll never forget the day I did ten chin ups off the eleventh floor fire escape of the old Minnesota Mutual Insurance Building.

It was like the President said, there are times when you have to weigh the rewards of success and the penalty for failure and just do what you gotta do.

Chapter Ten – Orbit
The difficulties of life are intended to make us better, not bitter.

Orbit was a Polish kid from Wisconsin and always seemed to be in orbit over something. He was sort of scatter brained and was always forgetting tools on jobs and would have to go back for them.

Orbit, which was the only name most of the crew knew him by, was going to night school like me.

He went to classes at the University of Minnesota, while I went to The American Institute of the Air the radio announcer school. We took a lot of ribbing about thinking we were better than everyone else, trying to get educated and everything, but I think most of the guys were secretly sort of proud that some of their own were going to school and were going to be somebody.

It was like they could imagine it was them and that they weren't really going to spend the rest of their lives as janitors and window cleaners but would get an education and a good job too.

It was like seeing someone else doing it, made it possible for them to think they could do it too.

Most of them would say stuff like, "Well as soon as I get a different car I'm going to get started over at Dunwoody," which was a big vocational school in Minneapolis, "or one of them schools, then I'll get a better job, and get off these buildings."

I think they knew deep inside they wouldn't, but it made them feel better to think they would. Orbit and I always agreed with them that it was something they would get started on, someday.

Well, Orbit, was a character. Big and raw boned, with hair that never stayed down but was always flying even though he used Wildroot Cream Oil or some other stuff on it. He had the look of someone who was never quite aware of what was going on, or where he was. Sort of like the absent minded professor. He was always looking for a squeegee or sponge or brush he had mislaid.

The guys would get a little tired of waiting for him to run back up to the janitors closet of the last floor they had worked on to find the missing equipment, but most just shook their heads.

Orbit usually had a book of some kind with him and read it while his partner was taking a break at the nearest 3.2 beer joint. It was obvious that Orbit would make something of himself eventually if he could just remember where and when.

He became a window cleaner, instead of a window washer the day he and Black Bill were working the eleventh floor of the Merchandise Mart. Bill was working the inside and Orbit catching the outside. Bill heard a scream, and looked out to see Orbit hanging by his safety rope six feet below the window. One side of his belt had unhooked and he had taken a flop.

"Pilot error," Czech called it later.

But there was Orbit, swinging back and forth on his safety rope six feet below the window sill, ten and a half stories up in the air.

Scared to death and stammering in a frightened voice, Orbit called out for help.

"Buh, buh, buh, Billlll, puh, puh, puh, pull me up." Black Bill reached out to grab the rope and haul him up but as he started to pull on the rope, Orbit screamed again. "Buh, buh, buh, Bill, puh, puh, puh, pull me up."

Whether it was the desperation in his voice or the sight of the big polish kid swinging back and forth at the end of the rope while he stammered out his call for help, Bill had to laugh. He had a weird sense of humor. It sent him into gales of laughter. Every time he leaned out the window to pull on the rope Orbit would cry out again. The stammering cry for help would send Bill into gales of laughter again and he would be unable to pull the big kid up the side of the building to safety.

Office workers were clustered around every window on the floor trying to see what was causing the commotion.

It must have been a sight to see.

After what seemed like an eternity to Orbit, two office workers came over and gave Bill a hand.

By then he was laughing so hard they thought he was hysterical. Together they hauled Orbit up the rope and back in the window. Orbit sat down on the floor, had a couple of smokes, then disappeared into a bar down the street and wasn't seen for a couple of days.

The next time they worked together Blind Bob said "What a team, Stuttering Sam and Babbling Bill. Let's see if we can keep both ends hooked today guys."

Black Bill thought it was hilarious but Orbit just stomped out and went to work.

I asked him later why he didn't just climb up the rope instead of waiting for Bill to pull him in.

He said he didn't know. He couldn't remember most of what had happened. I could relate to that.

That's what I did though, when I took the dive off the Empire Bank Building on North Robert. I just climbed the rope and got myself back in the window.

Czech came over that night and said, "So you took a flop from a building today huh? Well you know what we always say, when you've lived through your first fall you're a window cleaner, instead of a window washer."

I'd never heard anyone say that but I was secretly sort of proud that I had taken a dive like most of the rest of them and was now a window cleaner instead of a window washer.

I didn't tell the rest of the crew how scared I had been. I got the feeling that most of them had been there at one time or another and had a pretty good idea of how I was feeling.

And it was noted by the old guys that I climbed right back out the next window, and didn't use my fall as an excuse to disappear into a tavern for a few days.

Chapter Eleven - Orbit Comes To the International

Turn your wounds into wisdom. Oprah Winfrey

Our time with the President was growing short. The news conference set up by Jody Powell to help small town news reporters gain access to the federal government was to have been 45 minutes, but when an aide stood and said "Thank You Mr. President," he was waved off by a president who was apparently having a good time visiting with small town folks and wanted to continue on for a few more minutes.

A small town Virginia reporter asked about the breakdown of family values. "Is there anything government can do or should to help restore these values?" he asked.

I thought about Orbit, the Polish kid who knew all about dysfunctional families. He was attending night school at the university, and planned on becoming an accountant.

Joe and I would always remember that spring day he came to the International.

It was cold for March, with the wind from the river sweeping over Kellogg Boulevard and on up Wacouta Street to where we were cleaning the windows on the Greyhound Bus Depot. The diesel engines on the buses idling in the parking area created a film on the windows that required plenty of the cleaning agent tetra sodium phosphate or TSP as it was called.

We were cleaning the first floor plate glass on the store front next to the depot when the door swung open and this tall skinny teen ager walked out into the cool March morning. He was wearing clothes designed for a warmer day and shivered as he looked around, trying to adjust to his whereabouts.

He spotted us cleaning the windows and half turned as if to go the other way, but then with a scared but determined look on his face he walked up to where I was scrubbing down a window. In a voice that shook and sounded real scared he said, "Where can a god damn man get a god damn job in this god damn town?"

Joe looked up quickly when he heard the cursing and swearing.
This was not the type of language used in public by even the worst of the crew and not what you expected from a high school kid on a downtown street corner. As I started to tell the kid I didn't know of any jobs open at the moment, Joe stepped over and said, "Well Mister Del, I think it is time for a coffee break. Why don't you invite your new friend along so we can talk about the job Mister Frank has open at the International."

Well, he wasn't my friend, at least not yet, but if Joe wanted to buy coffee I was game. Normally we didn't stop for coffee once we got going but kept on working so we could take a longer lunch break.

At the coffee bar inside the depot Joe immediately set out to learn more about the kid who still looked scared to death, despite the friendly tone of voice Joe was using.

"What's your name and where are you from?" asked Joe.

"Me?" The skinny kid said, "Me I'm from Wisconsin, the Fox River Valley and the names Peter, Peter Orbitoski."

"Well what brings you to St. Paul Mister Peter Orbitoski?" asked Joe, "You look like you should still be in school."

"I had a problem with my dad and had to leave town" he answered, "and I don't have much money and need some kind of work right away."

"Hey Mister Del, with all the spring storm window cleaning coming up Frank will need another man for the downtown area, perhaps Peter will be the one."

Ever cleaned a window Peter?" I asked, and the shake of his head indicated this was not one of his marketable skills.

"Then here's what we will do," said Joe, as if the entire matter was already settled in his mind. "As soon as the coffee is finished we will take Peter outside and have him help us clean a few windows, then when Frank asks if he has ever cleaned any windows he will be able to say "Yes I have cleaned a few."

"How about it, Peter, you want to be a window cleaner?"

"You mean, you'll show me how to wash windows and your company will give me a job?"

"Well the first thing you'll have to learn is that we don't wash windows," I said. "Anyone can wash a window but it takes a professional to clean one. When you talk to Frank tell him you've cleaned a few, not washed a few, or he'll spot you in a minute."

It worked too.

Joe and I helped him clean a few windows, showed him the tools we used, the brush, sponge, chamois cloth, and the different sized squeegees. Joe showed him the moves a professional uses to clean a plate glass window without lifting his squeegee from the glass. That way all the dirty water ends up in one corner of the window where the sponge is waiting to sop it up before it can stain the bricks under the window or the sidewalk.

We told him what to say, and mainly what not to say, and how to act when the crew called him skinner. After the quick course, Joe thought he was ready to face the boss.

Joe had a lot of kids and I guess it wasn't hard for him to spot a scared teen aged kid who needed a little help in a new city and in a new life. But that's just the way Joe was. He had more than understanding about things like that. He had feeling for them. Had compassion for people who were hurting. It showed in everything he did and said. Joe was the kind of guy that should have a lot of kids. He must have been a great dad.

Frank looked a little puzzled when we brought the skinny kid into the shop with us that evening, and looked first to Joe and then to me for an explanation. He didn't learn much from us though and talked at length with Orbitoski to try and learn more about him. He didn't learn much about the kid's home or his problem with his dad.

Orbit knew how to work though, and caught on fast to the truck route procedure. Frank wouldn't allow him to work the buildings or the swing stage and kept him on the ground instead. He more than earned his keep.

Nearly a year passed and Peter Orbitoskis' name had been shortened to Orbit by the crew, and he had passed his GED tests, gotten his high school diploma and enrolled in the university night school before we learned much about him. When we did it came out in bits and pieces.

Orbit, that is, Peter Orbitoski was 17 the day he left home, and showed up at the Greyhound Depot in St. Paul.

He said his hard drinking father had beaten on him and his older brother until the older brother had left home, and Peter was left to take the full brunt of an abusive father's beatings.

On the day he left, Peter said, he had come home from high school baseball practice and walked in on a family argument during which his father had slammed his mother to the floor. Peter said he stepped in between them only to get slammed against the wall himself by his father who was in a rage. That was his father's mistake however, since he didn't notice the baseball bat his son had carried home from batting practice.

He apparently never did see it because as he turned from Orbit to take another swing at his wife, Orbit swung the bat.

He said he would never forget the crunching sound of the bat hitting his father on the back and side of his head, and of the blood that spurted from his ear, and how he didn't cry out or make a sound as he fell toward the floor.

"Leave," his Mother had said, "Here, take the money from his wallet and leave, don't come back or he'll kill you. Please don't come back just leave and take care of yourself Peter."

Orbit said he took the money his Mother handed him, kissed her on the cheek, jumped in the family car which he abandoned a block from the bus depot. He said a bus with the engine running was standing in the driveway and he shouted to the driver to wait for him. Running inside to the ticket window he asked where the bus was going and when the ticket agent said St. Paul he told her that's where he was going too. He bought his ticket, jumped on the bus and many hours later walked into a cold Minnesota morning. Joe and I were the first people he met.

Because of Joe, Orbit had a job and was able to take care of himself. He was only a year or so younger than me, but he apparently hadn't had a lot of life's experiences and went around for those first few months with a scared look on his face and would jump at every sound.

He gradually settled down, and that's when he went to the school authorities to ask about a high school diploma and how to get started at the University. His determination to get an education had been planted by his mother's desire to make sure he wouldn't turn out like his father.

By the end of his second year at the International Orbit was well on his way toward the accounting degree and was trying to figure out how he could get work at night so he could become a full time student at the university and get the degree faster. That's when he met Rose.

It didn't creep up slowly or come on a little at a time. It happened suddenly, overnight really, that he began to be even more forgetful of his tools or about the job we were doing. One afternoon as the crews came in and began putting their tools away for the day Czech called Orbit into the back room to discuss his carelessness and forgetfulness with the tools.

For Czech to call someone into the back room was a major event and everyone quieted down to hear what was going on.

Orbit, it seemed, had left a ladder standing on a sidewalk after he was through with a job and someone had run into it while they were hurrying out of the store and not watching where they were going. Even though they should have been looking where they were going, the ladder should never have been left in place with no one around it.

"It's getting worse every day," said Czech with rising voice, "It was bad enough when your forgetfulness caused everyone else to wait for you while you went back for your tools, but we cannot risk a law suit from someone who gets hurt by your not paying attention to what you're doing. Now what's going on, what's happening to you? Is it the school? Are you staying up all night to study so you can't stay awake during the day? Whatever's going on has to come to a stop now, right now. Do you understand?"

"I'm sorry Czech, you know I wouldn't do anything to hurt Frank or the International, and I have been staying up late, but not to study."

Czech said later a light went on inside his head. "It's a girl ain't it? It's a girl that's got you mooning around here so you can't even remember your name. It's a gosh dang girl ain't it?"

Orbit's head slowly nodded up and down and the sheepish look on his face turned into a grin. "She's wonderful Czech," he said, "She's really wonderful, I've never known anyone like her. She goes to night school too. We met in class and we've been going to the Ice Cream Parlor after classes to talk. I wish you could meet her Czech, she's really something."

Well there it was. A girl. Orbit had fallen in love, and had become even more absent minded. He never could seem to remember things but now with this wonderful girl on his mind he was really having problems.

"I should have known," said Czech, and the look of disgust on his face was plain to see. "I should have known there would be a girl behind this.

Hasn't anyone told you that with your school and your job you don't have time for this nonsense? Now listen to me boy and you listen good. This job requires your attention, and we aren't about to jeopardize our company or our customers because some girl has you twisted around her little finger and has you jumping through hoops for her. You get a handle on it boy and you do it right now or don't bother to come in tomorrow morning. You hear me Orbitoski?"

Orbit heard all right, and so did the entire crew. There was no mistaking the disgust in Czech's voice when he walked away shaking his head. "A girl, I should have known it was a girl."

It didn't seem to faze Orbit though. He just kept that big grin on his face and everything else seemed to roll right off.

He did concentrate on his job though and he did try to remember his tools and the job slips that were handed him each morning as he headed out for the days run.

He didn't talk much about his girl, other than to tell anybody who asked that she was really great and that was it. He never said who she was or anything else about her, which did keep most of the crew guessing.

Fall came and with it the cold of sun shortened days and also the new school year. Orbit with the new goals and motivation of having someone to share the plans for the future with talked at length about school and his plans for a future in accounting or banking. For most of the crew plans were made one day at a time, if any plans were made at all. The future was some nebulous thing that was either planned for us by the high mucky mucks or would take care of itself. They didn't quite understand Orbit's need for making something of himself and couldn't quite grasp this thing about setting goals and then working and studying to reach them. Orbit had motivation, and whether it was something instilled in him by a battered mother or by the love of a girl, it was there and he worked hard at his job and his school.

School had been in session for several weeks, and October's early sunset had arrived, darkening the shop and office areas of the International the day Orbit's girl walked in the door.

But she didn't come to see him.

As the door opened both Joe and Orbit looked up, then jumped to their feet, saying almost in unison, "Rosita, what are you doing here?"

Of course with Joe it was Rosita, with Orbit it was Rose.

The teen aged girl gasped and clasped her hand to her mouth while a look of consternation played across her face.

"Papa, Peter, you are both here, I didn't know," and with that her voice trailed off leaving the two window cleaners staring at each other.

"Orbit, you know my Rosita? How do you know her? Rosita, you did not tell me about this man. You know what I have said about these men in this business."

"Joe, I didn't know!" said Orbit, "Rose is your daughter and I didn't know, but that's great, I have been taking Rose out for ice cream after class. Why didn't you tell me Joe was your father Rose?"

Rose didn't answer however, just spun around and fled toward the door calling back over her shoulder "Mama couldn't come to get you Papa, she was late getting supper, and she sent me instead."

And then she was gone, the door swinging shut behind her as she fled to the car.

"Peter," Joe shouted, "My daughter will not go out with a man who cleans windows. She is too young to hear the language and the rough talk. She goes to church and will not be part of this kind of life of drinking and going to taverns every night. You will not see her again. You will stay away and I mean this Orbitoski! You will stay away from my Rosita."

Joe's words carried all the authority of a father worried about his daughter and there was no question in anyone's mind that Orbits romance was over.

"I don't understand," Orbit said to nobody in particular, "I don't understand. Why would Joe say these things? We haven't done anything but go to the Ice Cream Parlor after class, why would he object to that?"

We all knew why though. Every member of the International crew knew exactly what was going through Joe's mind, and could understand his violent reaction to the scene we had just witnessed. Rosita knew too. She must have known all along and that's why she didn't tell Orbit where her father worked and why she never mentioned Orbit to her family.

I guess we had all nearly forgotten that night two years earlier when the 16-year-old Rosita, with her newly earned driver's license had driven the family's ancient station wagon to the International to pick her father up after work.

When she walked into the shop Joe was still in the back room cleaning and putting away his tools so Gorgeous George, never failing to seize an opportunity to make a pass at anything that wore skirts headed for the front door where she was waiting for Joe.

What he said to her was not exactly clear to the rest of us since they were in the front and we were all back in the shop area. Whatever it was it caused her to shrink back away from him. Joe, entering the shop from the side door was just in time to hear the last few words and see Rosita's reaction.

With all the fury of a father whose daughter's honor has been insulted Joe spun George around and with one swing of the massive arms sent him up in the air and against the wall.

With one huge hand at his throat and one clutching the front of his shirt the dazed window cleaner was shaken like a rag and thrown toward the back of the shop.

Czech and the Hungarian jumped in at that point and got between the two trying their best to hold the angry father away from George.

"I didn't mean anything, I didn't mean anything," George cried out, as he fled through the back door to the alley and made his getaway.

"You will none of you ever speak to my daughter again," shouted the usually taciturn Mexican, "You will not insult her like that ever."

Czech tried to calm him down and tried to explain that none of the rest of the crew would say anything untoward to his daughter but Joe would have none of it. His daughter had been insulted by rough language from the meanest member of the crew and he was hot.

It was over a week before a shifty eyed and obviously hung over, not so gorgeous George, came back to work. And he stayed as far from Joe as the limitations of the shop and the morning bull session would allow.

Frank the Boss took him into the office that first morning back and they had a short but decisive visit.

He then called Joe into the office and explained that his daughter would never have to worry about being bothered by George again if she came to pick him up.

Joe said he understood but that was the last time anyone had seen Rosita, until the moment she had entered the room and found the two men she obviously cared for most, sitting almost next to one another in the shop.

Czech explained to Orbit as gently as he could why Joe had reacted as he did, causing Orbit to take a scathing look at George, before saying, "You! You did this to Joe and Rose and now I've got the problem. I oughta repeat what Joe did two years ago."

George beat a hasty retreat leaving Orbit to figure out what he could do to convince Joe he had only honorable intentions where his daughter was concerned.

Weeks went by with Frank trying to keep Joe and Orbit working on different jobs which was difficult since they were both on the building crew and normally would have worked together on a building at least once every week or so. They didn't talk about Rosita. As a matter of fact they rarely spoke during the morning bull session despite the fact that Joe had been a special friend since that day we first met Orbit fresh off the bus from Wisconsin.

The school year passed and a Minnesota springtime had arrived with its light breezes off the river thawing the dirty snow piles in the parking lot corners.

Orbit had completed two full years of night school and was searching for a night job so he could go to school full time days.

In late May as the semester ended he found his answer.

While cleaning the top floor of a bank building he overheard the personnel people talking about an opening the bank had on the night crew which cleared checks that came in during the day. Orbit took off his safety belt, put down his bucket and asked them if they needed someone with an accounting background. The personnel people, skeptical at first, heard him out as he explained that he would soon have two years of night school behind him. He said "I need to find a night job paying enough to let me to go to school full time to get my degree in accounting.

He said later they asked sharp questions and he didn't remember exactly what he had replied, but it must have been enough to get him the job. He would start as soon as he finished the semester of night classes.

We all thought his attitude was a bit strange during those next couple of weeks. He had seemed to enjoy his work at the International, and his association with the group of misfits who spent evenings on the bar tour and days recuperating.

The sad look he had worn for weeks, since the night Rosita came to the shop had disappeared and he seemed to look forward to leaving. More than you would normally expect. As if he could hardly wait to leave.

We thought it was because he was looking forward to working in a bank and going to school full time that brought about this change from the hang dog look he had carried since the encounter with Joe and Rosita.

The weeks passed, school ended, and he was gone to his new job and to prepare for a future as an accountant.

He left on a Friday, and the following Monday evening he was back. This wasn't unusual since nearly everyone who left the International, for whatever reason, usually came back to visit, only not usually this quickly.

He looked nervous and didn't seem to be as excited as he had been on the Friday afternoon when he left. This time however, he headed straight for Joe and said, "I would like to discuss something important with you Joe. Do you have a minute?"

Now it was Joe's turn to be surprised. Orbit hadn't talked to him a lot in the weeks since their encounter over Rosita.

"You told me," said Orbit, "you would never allow your daughter to go out with a window cleaner and I honored your decision. Now I am no longer a window cleaner. I work in a bank at night and attend accounting school during the day. I am now going to take your daughter out for ice cream after class and to movies and to activities at the University."

It was not a question, it was a statement. A statement made with as much authority and conviction as Orbit could muster up.

An almost audible gasp went through the shop as the crew waited to see if Joe would go after the young man who dared defy him. Czech and Jamie Kennedy moved closer as though their minds were running on the same wave length and they would stop any fireworks before they began.

Joe was startled, and looked at the floor for a long time before looking Orbit in the eye and saying, "Is that so? And what does my Rosita have to say about this? You have talked to her about this I suppose."

Orbit turned toward the front window and with an almost imperceptible nod brought the waiting girl in the front door.

"Why don't you ask her Joe" Orbit replied, "We came together to talk to you about this but I did not want her to see what happened if you objected as you did the last time. I asked her to wait outside."

"So, Rosita, you will go out with this window cleaner?" asked Joe.

"No Papa, I will not go out with a window cleaner, but I will go out with this banker, and I wish for you to say it is okay."

Joe had known the answer before he asked the question.
It was in their eyes. It was in the way they looked at each other.
We could all see it, and so could Joe.

"Well, Mister Banker," Joe said slowly, "I think it is time for you to come home with my Rosita so the rest of the family can see this university man she has waited so long for. Come on then, Mister Peter Orbitoski, I met you at the bus depot and helped you get the window cleaners job at the International. If I were your father I would be very proud of what you have done. Let's go home, Rosita. Let's take your banker home to meet your mother"

That Orbit. He was something. From a scared teenager running away from an abusive father, to a job in a bank and a girl who was willing to wait however long it took to solve the problems that kept them apart. He may have been scatter-brained and the name Orbit was probably appropriate since he always seemed to be in orbit over something but he sure made it come out right in the end. I guess everyone on the crew was happy for Orbit as well as for Joe and Rosita.

Everyone was a little quieter after the trio had walked out to Joe's car and were on their way home to meet the family.

This was a moment most of the members of this crew would never know. This moment of joy that comes to a man when he meets the girl who is exactly right. This moment of peace that comes when you know this is right and that nothing will ever come between you again.

Many of these men would soon be heading for the Pig's Eye Saloon to hang one on. Despite being happy for Orbit, there was a sadness in knowing that this moment would never be theirs. A sadness they would soon try to drown in cheap wine and rotgut whiskey. These were the substitutes for those innermost feelings of family. Those feelings of belonging to someone.

As the president spoke about family values I smiled at the memory of Joe and all his kids, and Orbit who, despite an environment of violence and poverty, held himself up to higher standards. Standards instilled in him by a mother who found herself in the position of being a victim. She apparently felt she had no way out, but offered her son a way out instead.

Wherever his strong family values and his Midwestern work ethic came from, they were easily discerned by Joe and by the rest of the crew.

I wondered to myself if the President had ever heard that quote from the former Secretary of Agriculture Ezra Taft Benson whose chair I was occupying at this very moment.

Benson said, "You can't get a person out of the slums, until you get the slums out of the person."

Chapter Twelve - Blind Bob

Mishaps are like knives. They either serve us or cut us. James Lowell

When it came to falling off the side of a building, nobody could equal the record of Blind Bob, one of the skinniest people I'd ever seen, with shoulders not much wider than his waist. He wasn't real tall, just skinny, as if eating too much had never been much of a problem at his house. He always wore blue chambray shirts and twill work pants. The guys ribbed him about shopping in the kids department at the newly remodeled Montgomery Wards Store out on University Avenue.

I think he really shopped in the men's department but his wife took big tucks in both the shirts and the pants to bring them down to his size.

One day while he was working five stories above the inside courtyard of the old Laurel Hotel he slipped through the leather safety belt and fell four stories to the roof of the hotel laundry. His safety belt and rope dangled from the bolts sticking out of the wall on each side of the window. Bob flew fifty feet through the air coming to a stop only after he had crashed through a skylight in the roof and into the laundry room. He said later he landed flat on his back on a table which was piled high with laundry being sorted by several women.

Glass flew everywhere from the shattered skylight. One of the ladies passed out in a dead faint.

As Bob put it, "She keeled over and disappeared beneath hundreds of sheets and pillow cases which were being sorted on the table." Those sheets, pillow cases and blankets flew in all directions, but not before they provided the cushion which gave Blind Bob a safe landing.

It bruised him up a little, but he wasn't bad hurt, only mad and worried about the jokes from the rest of the crew when they heard about it.

As soon as he got the laundry workers quieted down he called the office to get Frank to bring the insurance papers over to the hotel to cover the cost of replacing the shattered glass in the skylight.

He then went up the elevator and back to work.

The safety belt he had taken from the rack in the shop that morning didn't have enough holes to take up all the slack around his narrow waist.

A few minutes later his foot slipped on the ledge, he again lost his balance, and again went through the belt. This time he plunged through a skylight over the kitchen.

He landed on a table being used to prepare meat for the evening meal. He was knocked out by the rough landing and when he came to he was covered with blood. The ambulance crew wiped him off and discovered it wasn't his blood. Most of it was from the liver, steaks and hamburger the cooks had been preparing for dinner. The meat was now splattered on the floor and walls.

They took him to the hospital to check him out. He wasn't bad hurt, but they did keep him over night which made him indignant. He felt it lowered him in the eyes of the rest of the crew to have to stay in the hospital.

It worked out well though. When the doctors discovered that he was nearly blind in one eye and had a lot of vision loss in the other, they talked to Frank the Boss about checking out his eyes. They kept him for another day and had an eye specialist look him over.

After some surgery and new glasses he had much of his vision back.

He would look up at buildings and marvel at the white lines between the bricks, saying this was the first time he had ever seen them. In his whole life, he had never been able to see clearly and thought that it was just the way things had to be. Strange how things work out. He was mad about falling and it ended up opening a whole new world for him.

Later Frank made him foreman for the building crew. He was a new man, and no one ever beat his record of two flops in one day.

Chapter Thirteen - Mexican Joe

Accidents hurt - safety doesn't.

No one knew how long it had been since Mexican Joe came to St. Paul from Mexico, but he was a citizen of the USA and proud of it. He wore a little ceramic American flag on the front of his crumpled old bus driver's hat. Joe sent money to his mother in Mexico for years until he finally got her moved to St. Paul to live with him.

He had a big family, several kids, and was one of the few people on the crew who owned his own home.

It was just a small place on the south side but he had a garden and raised his own peppers.

My first day on the job he said "Come on, Mister Del, I will make of you a good window cleaner."

Sort of ticked me off. I thought I was pretty good already.

He didn't mean anything though. That's just the way he was, always ready to help.

Joe was small and stocky, with jet black hair, flecked with a few streaks of silver. He wore a mustache trimmed sharply in the style of Clark Gable and some of the other movie stars of the forties and fifties. He had wrists that were as big as most men's biceps and could hoist a forty foot wooden extension ladder around as if it were a toy.

Some of the others on the crew liked to work with the newer, lighter, aluminum ladders, but Joe always said he didn't trust anything as flimsy looking as they were. I think he was secretly rather proud of being able to handle the heavier, wooden ones.

He showed me the secret of carrying a fully extended wooden ladder. It was all in the balance, and it wasn't long before I could take a forty foot ladder that had been leaning against the wall of the building, and by balancing it just right, carry it, upright, to the next work site a dozen or so feet down the sidewalk. It was sort of fun as people, on both sides of the street would pause to see this towering ladder being carried by the skinny kid or the short, stocky Mexican guy.

   While working on the second floor of a downtown department store I carrying the fully extended forty foot ladder with a bucket full of water and tools hanging from the top rung. A blind guy walked in front of me.
It wasn't his fault. He couldn't see me. I didn't see him either. I was looking up at the bucket hanging on the top of the ladder.
The blind guy didn't get hurt, he just tripped me with his cane and as I stumbled I lost my grip on the ladder.

   Trying vainly to recover, I grappled with it, but was no match for the top heavy forty footer. It seemed to fall in slow motion and didn't spill a single drop of water from the bucket, until it hit the car.

   The distinguished looking gentleman at the wheel of the late model Lincoln was just waiting for the traffic light on the corner of Fifth and Waucouta to change. The ladder coming out of nowhere slammed into the hood of his car.

   Dirty water sprayed. The hood flew open. Something caused the horn on the car to short out so it began blaring. This drew the attention of everyone within a city block to the plight of the unsuspecting driver.

   Joe ran for a phone to call Frank the Boss who arrived at the scene moments later. By then the driver had worked himself into quite a rage. Frank got to put into practice everything he had ever learned about calming an angry customer.

   The police arrived sirens whining and lights flashing, and someone ripped the wires out of the Lincoln to silence the blaring horn.

   As the truck towed away what moments earlier had been a beautiful new Lincoln bystanders alternated between head shaking and giggling. Some were even rude enough to let loose with an outright guffaw over the hapless driver and the remorseful window cleaner.

   Later Frank laid down some new rules about carrying fully extended extension ladders up and down city streets during those hours that foot and car traffic were heaviest. He even started scheduling downtown jobs for 6 in the morning so they could be completed before the morning rush hour began. Some of the guys on the crew weren't happy about going to work so early, and let me know whose fault it was.

   Joe and I cleaned a lot of windows that summer He was proud to be working with someone who was going to be a radio announcer.

On a sunny afternoon, as we cleaned windows on the Lowery Medical Arts Building, I crawled in a window and found him explaining to a nurse that I was going to announce on radio.

It was pretty embarrassing when Joe turned to me and said "come on Mister Del, announce for the pretty lady."

I didn't know what to say, but finally mumbled the call letters of the school station KAIA, Minneapolis, St. Paul.

That's what they called the school station in those days, when the school was still the American Institute of the Air.

Then one night Brownie, Richard Brown, the owner of the school came to our class and announced that he was changing the name of the school to Brown Institute. With a big grin that made it sound like a joke he said he was tired of people calling to ask about his air conditioning repair course.

Brownie and his wife Helen were real inspirations to kids attending their school.

They both had polio long before Salk found the vaccine.

I think many of their students had greater handicaps than they did. The world couldn't see ours as easily because they weren't physical. They lay buried behind the "I'm as good as you are" face we showed the world, and the tough talk we used to keep the world of high mucky mucks at bay.

Our handicaps were nurtured by the years of trying to get by and trying to get ahead. And amplified by the looks we sometimes saw on the faces of the people for whom we worked in the buildings and stores. Joe was pretty pleased that I could "announce" for the pretty lady. He was a nice guy.

Chapter Fourteen - Ooftuh The Norwegian

If you're going through hell, keep going. Winston Churchill

"America is a neighborhood of the world," the president was saying, "A neighborhood made up of people from all corners of the world, who are now working together to build this nation." A building process that he said would never stop. It was a fine thought the President expressed, that people of all ethnic backgrounds, could come together to build a nation.

I almost told him I knew from firsthand experience just how true that was. How people, from every conceivable background, could indeed work together and could build a company as well as a nation.   But of course I didn't. I wasn't sure he or any of the other reporters there could have understood the type of background I would have shared with them. A background which included an upper mid-west Scandinavian upbringing. Scandinavians I found out came in many varieties.

Ooftuh was a Norwegian who spoke with an accent, even though he had grown up in this country. He lived around the Seven Corners area of Minneapolis near the intersections of Cedar and Washington.

"Snoose Boulevard" it was called in those days because so many Scandinavians lived there. They'd gather in the halls and taverns and chew snoose, which I thought was a really disgusting habit, but they played good music. Records by Ole Bull and his fiddle, Slim Jim and the Vagabond Kid, and by the many accordion players who lived in the area. The 3.2 beer joints, bars and taverns had many dances, festivals and Norwegian Lutheran smorgasbords. Of course Ooftuh never went to any of those. Like most of the others, he spent his free time in a neighborhood tavern drinking his 3.2 beer.

I didn't drink, so when we took a break in the afternoon I usually sat in the truck and read for an hour while they had their beer break. Often he would ask if he could borrow a quarter for a hamburger.

I'd say "No I don't have a quarter, but you can have half my sandwich if you want." He never took it though. He would always say "No I don't want to take your food."

Of course what he really wanted was a quarter for a beer but he would never say that.

One day Ooftuh, whose real name was Lars Larsen, with an "e", not an "o", as he always put it, was working with me on the old Northwest Bell Telephone Building. It was over 90 degrees. Very hot.

I was working the outside on the ninth floor which was used for storage rooms. The window I was cleaning stuck. I couldn't get it up and there I was, standing on a three inch ledge on the sunny side of the building. The windows and ledges were made of metal. They were hot. With the sun shining on them all day they seemed to soak up and reflect heat like a blast furnace.

We were supposed to carry a screw driver with us but mine was in the truck where I usually left it. If I carried it in my bucket I would stab my hand on it when I reached in for a sponge.

There I was nine floors up, on the sunny side of the street, and the metal window was stuck. I tapped on the heavy window glass with my squeegee to get Ooftuh's attention. He was supposed to be working right along with me on the inside.

As I went from window to window on the outside, he would do the same on the inside, but was usually a couple behind, since he had to work around desks, workbenches and furniture on the inside, while I had clear sailing down the outside of the building.

When you were working the outside and were ready to move to another window, you would grab the center of the window with the fingertips of your left hand, unhook the right side of the your safety belt and swing it over your left arm. The next step was to unhook the left side of your safety belt with your right hand and without letting go of the window hook the left side of your safety belt to the right side of the window. You would then step over to the next window, connect the right side of your belt to the left side of that window and reverse the unhooking process to get hooked up properly and be ready to clean the second window.

Although it sounds complicated, it was actually a quick and easy way to move down the side of the building.

Of course Frank the Boss always said go in and out each window, knowing full well that we all did crossovers because it was the fastest, easiest way to get the job done.

There I was, stuck outside on the ninth floor, in the sun, waiting for Ooftuh to catch up so he could open a window and let me in.

I had reached the last window and could go no further.

After 15 minutes, I finally did a crossover back to the last window I'd cleaned. No luck. It was stuck too.

This floor of the building was where thousands of round metal boxes held relays that switched calls. The thousands of relays chattered up and down in response to someone spinning a dial on a phone somewhere in St. Paul. It was loud. The rooms were not usually occupied. We were the only ones who ever opened the windows, and since we did crossovers all the way down the side of the building, none of the windows in the center had been opened for a long time. I waited another 15 or 20 minutes, tapping on the window with my squeegee handle and attracting no ones' attention. I then started doing crossovers across the side of the building toward the window I had climbed out of originally. It seemed like it took forever. A couple of times I got to wondering if I'd make it.

The heat was stifling; everything I tried to hang onto was made of metal and was burning hot to the touch.

By the time I reached the window I had climbed out of originally, an hour had passed. I had tried every window on the side of the building with the same results.

The heavy metal frames with fire glass, wouldn't budge.

Breathing a sigh of relief I finally got to the window I came out of and leaned down to open it.

It wouldn't move!

The window that had opened earlier with some difficulty from the inside, using the handles on the bottom to pull on, wouldn't move an inch, with the limited leverage I could give it with my fingertips up under the center of the hot, metal frame.

It had been over an hour in the sun now, and I was really hot. Not just from the sun either.

I was cursing Ooftuh, using even a couple of Swedish curse words I had learned listening to my Dad. At the point where I was ready to smash the glass he finally showed up looking cool and comfortable. He had spent the last hour taking his 3.2 beer break at a corner bar and couldn't see why I was upset or angry. All he did was take a little break for a beer.

It took a couple of Seven Ups to cool me down.

I took a magazine and headed for an empty room where I stayed the rest of the afternoon trying to cool off.

Chapter Fifteen - Black Bill

How good it feels! The hand of a friend. Longfellow

Black Bill could do crossovers better than just about anybody. He could balance on any size ledge and never seemed to lose control.

He had a weird sense of humor and played practical jokes on people. Not just on his fellow employees, but on people in the buildings where we worked.

On a summer day we were working on an old building housing a well-known home permanent company.

They had one room where a dozen ladies sat around a couple of long tables breaking off and counting little curlers. Those tiny home permanent curlers came from the plastic factory in long strings.

Their work room was on the tenth floor of the building.

There was a foot wide cornice about three feet below their windows.

Bill decided to play a little joke on the ladies who were enjoying the cool summer breeze coming in through their tenth floor windows.

Several rooms down from their work area he climbed out a window and onto the cornice. It was like a sidewalk for a man with Bill's agility.

He crept along the cornice, ten floors up in the air, until he reached a point directly below their open window. He waited for a moment until the good natured talking and laughing in the curler room had subsided.

When it was reasonably quiet he quickly stood up and let loose with a blood curdling scream that made Chippewa Charlie's war hoop sound like a babies cry.

Bill didn't mean anything by it but the sudden appearance of this apparition in their tenth story window caused the curler ladies to scream, jump up and tip over their table. Thousands of small home permanent curlers went flying everywhere, including many out the open windows. The small pink and blue curlers rained down on unsuspecting passersby ten floors below.

Frank the Boss was pretty mad when the home permanent people called to tell him they were canceling their contract and that he was going to have to pay for cleaning up the mess, and for all the curlers lost.

Fortunately, no one was hurt by the tiny home permanent curlers raining from the sky.

Bill disappeared for a few days until everything blew over. Later he apologized to Frank, but you could tell by the gleam in his eyes that he thought it was a good one. We could tell that Frank thought so too, because he never got really mad at Bill, just gave him a little chewing out because he knew he had to say something.

Czech said "Bill was a real wild man until a couple of years earlier when he got married. The ball and chain slowed him down some and he doesn't join us on the weekend binges anymore."

Bill had a couple of small boys and took them along when he cleaned apartment houses on weekends to help make ends meet. He rarely missed a day on the job and when he did disappear for a few days you knew it was pretty serious. We found out how serious on an early spring day. Dirty snow was still piled up in the alleys and the wind coming off the river was blowing cold. It whistled around the building crew when they were working ten or fifteen floors up on the Northwest Bell Telephone building on Kellogg Boulevard. It was this cold, damp air that started Bill coughing bad. He had a scratchy little cough as if he was trying to clear his throat in preparation for saying something but never saying it.

As he was working the shady side of the building he had a bad spell and began coughing up tiny flecks of blood.

Mexican Joe was the first to notice and after checking into the shop that night asked Frank if he could talk to him in his office. He told him about the blood and the coughing sounds and the grayness in Bill's face after a bad coughing spell. He said it was what he used to see back in Mexico when someone came down with what he called the coughing sickness. Here it was called Tuberculosis.

Frank took Bill aside and told him he wanted to take him to the company doctor for a checkup. This was unusual in itself. The company doctor was an old timer who kept office hours on the second floor of a building on State Street and usually saw International crew members for the occasional bruises or breaks from falling off a ladder.

This was different. Bill insisted that he was fine and that he just had a cold. He told Frank the damp weather made it worse.

Frank took him to Doc Moran anyway. The old doctor took one long look and ran him into the hospital for X-Rays.

No question about it. Black Bill had TB. Frank said it showed up clear on the X-ray. Bill knew, as everyone else did in those days, that when you got the coughing sickness, you didn't really have a choice, you went to a sanitarium for treatment.

Not just a long week end either. You could plan on being there for a long time.

Many months would pass as they kept you in bed and made you rest until their cure all's and medicines could do their work.

Bill was upset. His wife and two kids were in for a tough time without his wages and he knew it.

There weren't the safety nets many folks find today. No workers comp and very little unemployment compensation. Only welfare, and precious little of that.

He tried to convince Frank the Boss that he could keep working but Doc Moran told him it wasn't even a choice and that he was going to the Glen Lake Sanitarium whether he wanted to or not.

It was in the middle of the week, on a Wednesday when Frank and Bill climbed into a company truck and headed for the sanitarium at Glen Lake on the west side of the cities.

Bill's wife Bekka came to the shop Friday afternoon to pick up his last pay envelope.

It wasn't hard to tell that she had spent a lot of the last couple of days crying. With both Bill and his pay gone for a long time, and no way of knowing how long that would be, things were going to be tough.

Her eyes opened wide when she saw how much money was in the pay envelope Frank the Boss handed to her.

She said "Oh no, Mr. Frank, this can't be right, Bill only worked two days, and this is the whole week's pay."

Frank explained that he was paying Bill for the whole week as a bonus, but added, "You know Bekka, I would keep him on the payroll while he's at Glen Lake, but we just don't have that kind of money."

It must have been during their weekend binge that a couple of the crew started talking about what could be done.

81

They talked first about taking up a donation each week and giving the money to Bill's wife and kids.

That idea went over like a lead balloon. Most of the crew barely made it through the weekend on what their pay envelope contained each Friday.

Czech and Blind Bob figured out what they thought could be the best solution to Bill and Bekka's problem while they were sitting in the dimly lit back booth of The Pig's Eye Saloon during the weekend.

First thing Monday morning they ran their idea by Frank to see if he thought it would work.

He said it sounded good to him to and asked the rest of the crew if they would give it a try.

"Each week as long as Bill was gone," Frank explained, "or as long as it seemed to be working, I'll take forty hours' worth of job slips and put them in a box on the counter. These will be the job slips Bill would normally have each week."

The crew members would then take one or two of the job slips each day, and fit them in on lunch hours or during the time they would normally be taking their coffee or 3.2 beer breaks.

Frank added, "If this works, Bill will get his forty hours of work and Bekka can stay off welfare and get by until Bill gets back home."

Everyone on the crew agreed they would try and do forty hours of work for Bill during their regular work week.

"If it doesn't interfere with your regular jobs, and I don't get any complaints about windows being skinned, it's okay by me." Frank told the crew that first morning. "Lets' give it a shot."

By Thursday afternoon Bill's forty hours of job slips had been taken care of by the crew.

Frank called Bekka and said, "Come on by the shop this afternoon about four thirty. We'll have a surprise for you."

The whole crew was in and had their tools cleaned up and put away when she walked in carrying one of the boys and pulling the other alongside.

Czech explained what they had done. How they had each taken a couple of the job slips Bill would normally have had and fit them in to their schedule during the week.

"Bill," Czech explained, "got his forty hours in for this week and we will try and get his hours in each week until he is well enough to come back to the International." And he added with a grin, "You can tell Bill the windows are cleaner than ever and we found the ones he had skinned by the week before," but added, "I'm just kidding Bekka, just kidding."

Bekka looked bewildered as if she wasn't quite sure what he meant until Frank handed her the full pay envelope.

He said, "stop by each Friday afternoon and we'll have Bill's regular pay for you."

The look on her face was something to see. I know it doesn't seem like much now, but it was obvious that the eighty bucks in that pay envelope was like being handed the world. She knelt down by the kids, and with tears streaming down her cheeks said "We can stay in our house kids. We can stay in our house. We don't have to move to Aunt Janie's after all."

Standing up she threw her arms around Czech's neck which turned several shades of red at this unexpected display of gratitude. As she planted a big kiss on the wrinkled old cheek most of the others turned away to avoid being the recipient of any further outbursts of appreciation.

It was an unusual form of public assistance. But when life has you down and out, you go for whatever works.

"Bekka," said Frank, when things quieted down, "How are you going to get over to Glen Lake to see Bill?"

The Glen Lake Sanitarium for tuberculosis sufferers was clear over on the west side of the cities and some fifty miles from where Bill and Bekka lived on the East side of St. Paul.

"I don't know" she said, "I just don't know."

"Can you drive?" asked Frank.

"Yes, but we have no car. We take the streetcar or bus."

Frank said, "I have an extra key for the old truck in the shop. You can pick it up when you come for the pay envelope on Fridays but we have to have it back Sunday afternoon so we can use it on Monday morning."

It was a put together relief program with everyone just trying to help someone else get by and it worked.

It was many months before Black Bill was back on the job, thinner, but looking better than he had for a long time.

The unexpected weekly pay provided by his co-workers and the use of the International's old truck seemed to carry the family through.

"From early spring to late fall," Bill told the crew later, "Bekka and the kids drove over Glen Lake every Saturday morning and spent the day with me. It was the highlight of every week when that old company truck pulled into the parking lot."

As the sun went down and evening came on they would spread bedrolls out in the back of the pickup truck. There, under the stars, or under a piece of canvas if it rained, they slept.

They spent nearly every Saturday night in the back of the truck so they could see Bill again on Sunday morning. Then on Sunday afternoon they would begin, what was for them, the long drive home. It was only fifty miles but that was a whole world away from the area of the cities they lived in. A long trip for a family not used to traveling further than they could walk or take the bus.

Black Bill was different when he came back. I wasn't the only one who noticed it either.

His first day back on the job, the usually fun loving practical joker tried to find words that would tell this hard-drinking, party loving crew how much he appreciated what they had done. Finding the right words would have been hard under any circumstances.

With the bantering of the crew flying around the newly returned skinner it was almost impossible. But they knew what he meant.

He was different though. It was in the way he looked around. In the way he talked. He still played an occasional practical joke, but even when he was laughing the flash was gone. There was no humor in his eyes. They were serious. Not angry, or anything, just serious. As if he was unable to look at the world the way he had in the past.

While we were working on the NP Railroad building one day I asked Mexican Joe what he thought it was.

"He can't be the same now Mister Del. He can never be the same now that he is an important man."

I said "Whatta ya mean important, what makes him more important now than he was before the TB?"

"Oh no! It is not the coughing sickness or the sanitarium that makes him important. It is because he now has friends. In the past Bill was just like everyone else. Now everyone on the crew did him the great kindness. They did his work and provided for his family. Now they are his friends. When a man has friends that makes him important."

Joe had an answer for everything and his explanation for Bill's seriousness made sense to me.

"Sometimes," said Joe, "people think money makes them important. Sometimes when they are high mucky mucks in the city or the county they think that makes them important. But when you have friends, that's when you are important. When others care about you then you have to care about them too. That's why our friend Bill is more serious. He always had friends, but before the coughing sickness he didn't really know it. They worked with him, got drunk with him, laughed with him, but they didn't provide for him and his family. Now he knows, he has friends. It's an important responsibility and one he has never had before."

It was a long speech but seemed to hit the nail on the head.

Orbit said Bill had even asked him about night school and what he would have to do to get enrolled at Dunwoody Institute, the vocational school in Minneapolis.

And that's what happened.

He enrolled in the welding program at the vocational school and began his move upward into the real world.

After graduating from Dunwoody Bill went to work for Indianhead Trucking Company as a welder, making more money in a week than he did in three as a skinner at the International.

He stopped by a couple of times when he was working the night shift at Indianhead, and joined in the morning bull session.

The men who had pulled him through the tough times were glad to see him, but it wasn't like the old days. Black Bill had worked hard to put himself through the vocational school and had earned his new job, his new found wealth, and his new life. The guys were glad to see him and eager to ask questions about the job, but were always a little quiet after he left. As if they were thinking to themselves, they could do that. They could go to Dunwoody and get a good paying job.

They knew they could, and probably would, but of course this wasn't the right time. Maybe next fall when the new school year got underway, perhaps then they could start, but of course they never did.

Chapter Sixteen - Clyde and The Swing Stage

While on a ladder, never step back to admire your work.

A swing stage is a scaffold that is lowered down the side of tall buildings so construction and maintenance crews can work on the exterior of the building.

Most window cleaning wasn't done that way in those days, but once in a while we were called on to paint scrape some new construction, and would work on the scaffold or swing stage.

Clyde was a big man. His real name was Gerald, but he was so big the guys called him Clydesdale after the large work horses the farmers used in the Minnesota State Fair horse pulling contests.

By the early fifties when I came to work at the International the nick name had been shortened to Clyde.

Clyde towered above everyone else on the crew. He had a barrel like chest, and a stomach that had been the recipient of plenty of beer and food. He sported a thick brush of a mustache and wore his hair long which gave him the image of a mountain man or lumberjack.

Clyde was known for his appetite and had the stomach to prove it. He also had a voice that was both deep and loud. He could have sung bass with a barbershop quartet but would probably have drowned out the other three voices, especially if he had been fortified with a few ounces of his favorite booze.

Clyde feared nothing and nobody but like many really big men nobody feared him either. He seemed to understand the damage he could cause to his fellow human beings and treated everyone with what passed for gentleness.

On a sunny mid-summer day Clyde was paint scraping a building in downtown Minneapolis. He and Sir Winston stood on the swing stage and scraped the paint and putty that remained on the windows after the building construction had been completed. Paint scraping was a tedious job which required close attention and required cleaning not only the windows, but the metal on the areas between floors as well. Each "drop" down the side of the building took several hours.

They would clean a segment of the side of the building then untie the knots that held the swing stage in place and lower it a few feet to a new area of the building. At each stop they would clean an area the length of the stage and as high as they could reach and would then begin the process of lowering the scaffold a few feet before tying it off with a couple of big knots.

I never did learn how to tie off a stage right so nobody wanted to work the swing stage with the Herring Choker. That was all right with me because that was one place I was really nervous about working.

I was on the ground feeding the long ropes up the side of the building and keeping the sidewalk blocks in place while Clyde and Sir Winston worked their way slowly down the side.

I had the gravy job with plenty of time between moves. The two men came slowly down the side of the building scraping paint and putty as they went. As the swing stage came down, the rope went up uncoiling from its place in the big 55 gallon barrels. The metal drums sat immediately below each end of the scaffold. The rope coiled neatly in the barrels as the scaffold was raised, meant it wouldn't snag as the stage came back down on the next drop.

Clyde had big fingers and was known to have a little problem getting the heavy rope tied into a good stiff knot at each stop.

Midafternoon, with the sun shining down it was hot and the guys were in a hurry to get down so they could take a 3.2 break. The rest of the crew would move the stage and set up for the next drop.

I heard a scream, and before I could move, ropes started flying in the air and the barrel, a few feet from me, turned over with a loud bang. I heard cursing and swearing coming from behind the barrel.

It was Clyde. Clyde who was supposed to be five and a half floors above scraping paint and putty had apparently missed the knot. He didn't get it tied tight. It slipped and his end of the stage had dropped out from under him. He went flying five floors through the air, leaving Sir Winston hanging on for dear life to the ropes on his end of the swing stage which was now hanging vertically down the side of the building. Cursing with ever increasing volume Clyde climbed slowly out from behind the barrel and the tangle of rope.

There he stood, glaring at the mess, without even a thought to the fact that he could have died falling that far. All Clyde could do was curse the luck that he felt caused his downfall.

Passersby, construction workers, and people working in the offices of the building stared in amazement at the huge man. They listened as he used all the curses he had ever heard and probably some he made up on the spot.

As we later figured out, Clyde had missed the knot allowing the ropes to slide freely through the pulleys and dropping his end of the swing stage straight down. The other end had been properly tied by Sir Winston and stayed in place with Winston hanging on for all he was worth.

Clyde slid off the stage, flew fifty feet through the air and landed with one huge leg inside and one leg outside the barrel.

They were so far down the side of the building the barrel Clyde hit was about half full of rope. Rather than splitting the big man in two, the foot hitting the ropes inside the barrel a split second before the other one hit the ground caused the barrel to tip over, breaking his fall.

He was badly bruised, but nothing broken.

The ambulance crew arrived and looked over the scene of the great disaster, the ropes, the barrel, the cursing window cleaner and the second workman still hanging from the swing stage five floors above. When they heard that Clyde had landed with one leg in the barrel and one leg outside they looked astounded.

Then they looked at each other.

Then they laughed.

It wasn't really funny, the guy should have been dead. Window cleaners always said the insurance companies figured you were going to be killed if you fell from five floors or above, and that's where he was. He should have died or been bad hurt, but instead there he stood, bruised, battered and cursing. We finally lowered the stage and got Sir Winston down. Clyde was placed in the ambulance for a trip to the hospital. Sir Winston took off down the street to a 3.2 joint and had a couple of beers.

After Clyde got checked out at the hospital, the two of them disappeared for a few days.

Chapter Seventeen - Sir Winston

We understand death for the first time
when he puts his hand upon one for whom we care. Madame de Stael

Sir Winston was a nice guy who came from England after the war. The guys all kidded him about being a war husband.

At that time there were a lot of GI's bringing brides home from overseas and the newspapers called them war brides. Winston had fallen in love with a WAC he met while she was stationed near his RAF outfit in England during the closing months of the war.

When they got married they decided to live in the states, making him a war husband.

The crew got a big kick out of that.

Sir Winston was a nice guy and of course had a heavy English accent. People in the offices where we worked always listened in when he talked. You could tell he knew when some of the office workers were listening because he would always raise his voice a little.

Everybody called him Sir Winston, because he was English, and because to our ears he actually sounded like the great man.

Winston Churchill, we all believed, had stood up to the Nazis and their Luftwaffe throughout World War Two and we all thought he got a raw deal after the war when the English people bounced him out of his job as Prime Minister. People would ask Sir Winston why his people would do such a thing too such a great man. He loved to talk about it.

Sir Winston had a sort of gentlemanly look about him and had what passed for a "handlebar" mustache drooping off the corners of his mouth.

With sandy colored hair, and the mustache, which he twirled by the ends when he talked, he did look like what we believed an English gentleman would look like. Perhaps he really was a man who had known better times and better places in another lifetime. Life in Great Britain had been a little different for him prior to the war and the devastation it brought.

Hitler's buzz bombs had destroyed many a gentleman's business, leaving them to pick up the pieces after the war which is what Sir Winston seemed to be doing.

He hated working on ladders, and thought they were dangerous, much preferring the life of a building man where you hung safely from a belt locked securely into bolts on each side of the window.

It was one of the hottest days in July when Frank the Boss said "Winston I need you on a job over on the south side."

It was a car dealership in South St. Paul. Because of the stock yards and cattle slaughter houses all over that area the flies swarmed through the hot summer air like a cloud and kept windows black and dirty.

The stockyards were not pleasant places to work anytime of the year and in the last days of July and early August with the stench and the flies, it was not where anyone on the crew wanted to be. The windows would be so bad you had to climb up on a ladder and scrub them with a brush. At times we even used Hy Dee, hydrochloric acid to get them clean. This was dangerous stuff that would burn through clothing and into the skin if you got careless. Heavy rubber gloves saved the skin but made it hard to hang on to the brush and ladder.

The ladder we used was six feet tall and came to a point on top. We wrapped a towel around the point so it wouldn't scratch the windows.

Sometimes when the towel got wet, and soapy, from the tri-sodium phosphate we used in our water it got slippery.

We all liked to work fast and move on to another job when we were sent to South St. Paul and were moving at a pretty good pace this time too. The windows needed the full treatment with HyDee and TSP. The water in the buckets turned black after only a few windows and we were constantly refilling them with clean water.

Sir Winston was near the top of the ladder, stretching to reach the top of the window when the wet, slippery towel tied around the top began to slide across the glass. As the ladder slid it bumped the center frame on the window throwing Winston from his precarious perch.

He flipped over in the air and landed head first striking his head on the concrete block used to keep cars back from the side of the building.

He was dead before we got to him.

They called an ambulance, and Frank the Boss came.

The police and the coroner were there, trying to fix the blame, but Sir Winston was dead. They couldn't fix that.

It wasn't like when the Hungarian died. Winston had a life. He was married. He had family. He shouldn't have died.

We all missed him, and everybody sort of lowered their voices when they mentioned his name. His funeral service was held in a church with regular preaching and stuff. He was buried in a real cemetery instead of at The Ridges like the Hungarian. The entire crew was invited back to the church for tea and cakes in the basement meeting room afterwards. We didn't stay long though as most of us were ill at ease moving among the other mourners, most of whom seemed to be high mucky muck friends of Winston's wife. Besides, the crew members were all anxious to make the run to The Pig's Eye to hoist one in memory of the dearly departed. A tradition that was probably more for the living than for the dead.

Sir Winston was missed; he had come to America to find a new life and had succeeded in doing that until the swarms of flies from the stockyards in South St. Paul caused his demise.

Chapter Eighteen - Baling Cockroaches

Cockroaches really put my "all creatures great and small"
creed to the test. Astrid Alauda

I tried to concentrate on what the President was saying. He was seated a couple of chairs away at the end of the table. In an effort to reach the people of The United States, Press Secretary Jody Powell had set up these monthly news conferences for small town reporters. Giving them access to the Federal Government without having the news filtered through the networks and wire services.

"What about the young people of America?" Asked one reporter, "Where do they go for help in getting an education and a job?"

I could have told them about self-help and how I had once had a job baling cockroaches while working my way through school. It would have grossed them out. It was gross, but it was a job, and it was there when I needed it, and it helped us through the hard times.

And it did give me a good story to share with my kids when they thought they really had it tough.

Most of the crew hated to do janitor work. It was beneath the dignity of a real window cleaner. Once in a while Frank the Boss would bid on a window cleaning job and would have to bid on the building maintenance program too.

One such job was a building housing an art school in Minneapolis. Frank knew everybody on the crew hated this kind of job so he would have each of the crew members work it on a rotating basis. That way everyone had to take a shot at the building maintenance job. He had us all work a month at a time on the all night shift.

Along with cleaning the floors, vacuuming and dusting, we had to walk through the entire six floors on a regular schedule, and at certain times twist a "call button" which let the security company know that all was right in the building. The guys hated the job, and hated being night watchman for the dark, spooky old building, with its creaky floors and dark stairways. If they missed a security point check-in the company had to dock them a quarter, since the security company then had to call the building and find out what was wrong.

The security checks were sent in, but with a lot of grumbling by the guys who felt put out over having to maintain the regular schedule all night long. That meant they weren't free to take a 3.2 break at one of the late night honky tonks in the area of the art school.

The complaining stopped the night Bottle Bill opened the door to the freight elevator and stepped in, forgetting that he had walked down from the sixth floor to the fourth floor.

The elevator was still on six, as he found out when he stepped into the darkened elevator shaft and plummeted five floors to the basement. He landed in a tangle of cables, pulleys, wheels and metal braces at the bottom of the shaft. He ended up with a broken leg and broken ribs.

When he failed to make his security check the service called and failing to get an answer sent someone to the building to find out why.

Bill was awake and groaning at the bottom of the shaft so it didn't take them long to find him and get an ambulance.

He pulled through but was off work for months. That meant they were short of people for the night maintenance work and we each had to take an extra turn at the hated job.

I would get there at midnight and go through the first security walk through of the building twisting the call knobs in the proper sequence. Then it was time to get started on the cleaning.

About three in the morning I could no longer put off the worst job of the night and headed for the basement to bale paper.

We all called it the worst job with good reason. From all over the country people would send in the tests the art school sent out in response to their search for people with artistic talent.

The instructors would then grade the tests and lessons and throw them into a chute the size of a freight elevator. The chute started on the sixth floor and went all the way to the basement.

After finishing the cleaning jobs for the night I would head for the basement and begin the process of baling all the waste paper which had been dropped down the chute during the day. We used an old hand operated paper baler. It made bales about like those you see coming out of hay balers on the farm.

Baling paper doesn't sound like too bad a job, but what we hated wasn't the paper, it was what went with it.

When the big metal door at the bottom of the six story paper shaft was opened the paper would be stacked at least three or four stories high. As the door was pulled open the entire mass of paper would be rising and falling like the waves on an ocean.

Tens of millions of cockroaches called the shaft home and were moving the paper as they went about their business. As I opened the door the cockroaches nearest the opening spread across the floor like a carpet, trying to escape the bright light. They would rush headlong into the dark spaces under the baler. When I lifted my foot hundreds of them would rush under it to get in the shadow.

The next part was to take a big six prong pitch fork and shove it into the shaft of paper. Lifting a load of paper, and cockroaches, I would shove them into the opening of the baler. After three or four pitch forks full of paper and roaches I would turn the big wheel on the side of the baler. This would crunch the mass of papers together. I would turn the wheel backward to loosen it and the filling process would begin anew.

When enough paper and roaches were packed into the baler the wheel would get a final tightening turn. Wires were inserted into the sides, and twisted tightly so the bale wouldn't fall apart as it was deposited on the palette ready to be hauled away in the morning.

It was an unpleasant job and I think everyone on the crew breathed a sigh of relief when an out of town company underbid Frank and took the job away. I think he was secretly happy too.

It's always hard to lose a job but there are those times in life when it seems like no amount of money would convince us to do that one again.

As I said, the job did have one bright spot.

As our six kids grew and went out to find their first jobs, no matter how hard they had to work, no matter how dirty their job, they could never complain too much after they heard, once again, the story of my job baling cockroaches. Once, as we were eating dinner, one teenager began telling another about how hard they had worked that day.

The other answered, "Shh don't say anything or Dad will make us listen to the cockroach story again!"

They all laughed and to this day if one of their kids complains about doing a hard job they can always tell them not to complain or they'll ask Grandpa to tell them the cockroach story.

The cockroach job didn't last long, but even now, as I sit here in the White House listening to the President talk about the need for jobs, and job training, I think back to the nights spent twisting the security alarm knobs, walking through the spooky old building with its creaky, grease stained floors, and about baling cockroaches at three in the morning.

The president explained the necessity for government to help create jobs which would help people save their dignity.

A reporter asked what seemed like the obvious question. "Isn't dignity something each individual has to create for themselves because they have the desire to make it on their own?"

My mind was taking me back to a different age, a different time when people seemed to accept the responsibility of trying their best to take care of themselves before they went to the government for assistance.

It seemed like everything the President said reminded me of the many ways the skinners at the International had adapted themselves for survival in an alien world. A world that could be either harsh or helpful depending on how its residents perceived you, your intentions and your attitude.

Most of the street people I met had developed what they called the sixth sense necessary to read the look on your face, the tone of your voice and the body language that told them how comfortable or uncomfortable you were in their presence. They reacted accordingly.

It had been over twenty five years since my days as a skinner with the International, but the lessons on learning to live with people, regardless of where they came from or what color their skin happened to be were as fresh as if they had been learned today. We were men of every race and every ethnic background who now worked together, and depended on each other, often in dangerous places. Depending on one another for backup, and for the deeper support that was always there, but most often unspoken. Makes you wonder, doesn't it? If people from all over the world can come together, work together, trust one another, many times with their lives.

Why can't the governments of the world work together?

Chapter Nineteen - The Inspiration of Mexican Joe

We can do no great things, only small things with great love.
Mother Teresa

The crew of The International had apparently taught me a lot more than how to clean windows. Those lessons on race relations and ethnic backgrounds were more real than ever as the President spoke about the community of nations.

Had he visited us at the International during the morning bull session I'm sure he would have found his community of nations operating right there.

Most of them lived on incomes that would now be considered well below the poverty level. This didn't stop them from feeling compassion. It didn't stop them from offering a helping hand when one was needed and most often, doing it with grace and good humor.

Mexican Joe was the best example. In him the International had a man who could move from his world on the poor side of town to the walnut paneled board rooms in the skyscrapers, and do it with grace and dignity.

It was pretty rare to see Joe anything but happy. He always gave the impression that somewhere in his past he had known other feelings and was bound and determined he would never see them again. He always had a smile and some bit of philosophy about being happy to share with everyone he met. Customers of the International seemed to enjoy having Joe come around. Their own little corner of the world was often times a small cubicle several floors up in a downtown building. They had their job and perhaps it was not always an exciting one. They would work at it hour after hour, day after day, and the coming of Joe the Window Cleaner seemed to bring momentary respite from the monotony and added a bright spot to their day. They always seemed to look up with interest and a touch of excitement as he came whistling down the hall. He would open the window with a flourish and effortlessly climb out. There, standing nonchalantly on the window ledge he would quickly scrub away the grime of the citys atmosphere with his brush. Then with many a twirl and spin of the squeegee he would move the dirty water quickly back and forth across the glass bringing it together in the lower right hand corner where a sponge waited to soak it up.

It was a rare occasion when even one drop would escape to dirty up the window ledge or spray down on an unsuspecting bystander on the street far below. Joe was a window cleaner, not a window washer. He was a professional and was proud of his expertise.

One afternoon in late April when spring was coming fast and the sunny side of the building soaked up enough sun to make it just warm enough to be uncomfortable, the whole building crew took their afternoon break at the same time.

While a couple of the others on the crew were taking their traditional 3.2 beer break, Joe and I visited the coffee shop in the drug store on the first floor of the Lowery Hotel. Joe stopped in front of the window of the childrens' store located next to the drug store and looked long and with great interest at the collection of First Communion dresses.

"There is the one my Maria wants." he said, pointing to a beautiful white lacy dress. It was I suppose the dream dress of every little girl getting ready for the big day.

Although most of the members of the crew rarely mentioned family Joe was obviously proud of each of his many kids and could talk about them at length. It got to where you felt you knew them each by name and by their many talents.

For once Joe looked almost sad. "If I had the money, that's the dress," he repeated, "that's the dress my Maria wishes for."

Then brightening up a bit he said "But of course even if we don't have the money for that one, Mama will make her a fine dress, and Maria will look like an angel." With that he straightened his shoulders and with his cheerful whistle headed toward the elevator to go back to work.

I mentioned Maria's First Communion dream dress to Black Bill the next day. By morning everyone on the crew was talking about what could be done. What could we do about the dream dress for Maria's first communion?

The dress wasn't very expensive by today's standards but in the 1950's dollars we were earning it was a lot.

During a 3.2 break several members of the crew decided Maria should not be denied her dream and a collection was started, with the help of Frank the Boss who was sworn to secrecy.

Several of the guys ran an ad in the St. Paul Pioneer Press that announced professional window cleaners were available to take down storms and put on screens. Most professional window cleaners thought this was hard labor and not the kind of work window cleaners do. This effort seemed to emphasize how important they thought this project was. With a truck loaned by Frank they would go out each afternoon when they finished their regular job and would do the hot heavy work they hated; they would take off storm windows, clean house windows, and put on screens, but only this once, and only long enough to get Maria her dream dress.

Although the temptation to hit the nearest 3.2 beer joint after several hours of the hated hard labor must have been nearly overwhelming they dutifully brought Maria's money as they called it, into the shop the next morning. With lowered voices, so Joe wouldn't hear, they would turn it over to Frank.

On the Friday before Maria's big day Czech stopped by the store and looked in the window one last time to make sure the dress was still there.

When everyone was through for the day and had arrived back in the shop Czech with great dignity and much ceremony presented the envelope of cash to Joe. He announced with great pride, "Joe, your coworkers here at the International want your daughter Maria to have her dream, her beautiful First Communion dress."

Most of the guys turned away and adopted a "so what's the big deal" attitude, when tears started running down the swarthy Mexican's cheeks. He looked around and mumbled something in Spanish.

"Mister Frank, I must use the phone" he proclaimed as he literally ran toward the office. We knew his wife had answered when he shouted "Mama, Mama," and then the rest was a torrent of Spanish so fast that we doubted anyone, even Joe's wife could understand it.

Monday morning Joe asked everyone for silence so he could speak the gratitude of his family. It may seem like such a little thing to others but Joe knew the sacrifice the little envelope of dress money meant. He soon learned about the extra evening jobs taken on by several members of the crew.

Joe was unusually eloquent as he described the moment when his little Maria received her surprise. He did well in describing the laughter and the tears. He told her about the sacrifices and hard work of his co-workers which had changed the impossible dream to the possible dream.

He got real excited when he told the crew of hard drinking window cleaners how his Maria had nodded her head up and down and said repeatedly, thank you, thank you, thank you in both English and Spanish.

Joe had been a Skinner at the International for many years, but as he looked around the room at his coworkers that morning he seemed to understand for the first time that he was fully and completely accepted as one of them.

It must have been hard coming from Mexico, or any foreign country for that matter and starting a new life. Especially when your English was colored with a heavy accent, and was the subject of good-natured ribbing.

And maybe some that wasn't so good-natured too.

As I looked around at the crew that morning, it seemed as if their faces had softened. It appeared that the effects of years of booze and cigarettes weren't quite as pronounced. That the pride Joe felt in his little Maria was now also their pride. As if they, too, were once again part of a real family.

Maria's first communion dress had given the rough, tough hard drinking crew of the International one of those rare moments when they felt a real sense of family. Real pride of accomplishment. A feeling of sharing that wasn't always readily discernible in their daily lives.

Chapter Twenty - Don't Mess With The International

Lack of moral values can bring big pains in life. Treebranch

One day Frank the Boss came to the morning bull session and just stood there, shifting from one foot to the other, as if he wanted to say something but wasn't quite sure how to begin. Finally Czech said "Mornin' boss man, got some skinners for us today, everyone had a hard night."

This was a standard joke, since everyone knew that Czech did his work and never skinned a window.

"Well," Frank said slowly, "I received a couple of job cancellations this morning and was wondering about them. When I arrived at the shop this morning, before I even got my coat, off the phone was ringing and I got an earful from Jimmy Conners over at the 4th street hardware. When he got to his store this morning he found his plate glass windows were streaked and dirty. The morning sun showed off every streak. We were the ones who cleaned them yesterday."

Frank said, Jimmy thought the streaks were left by the International team and canceled our contract. He signed up with that new outfit that went into business a few weeks back. They just happened to call on him right after he opened for the day."

The Perfect Window Cleaning Company was started by a couple of guys who had arrived weeks before from Seattle. Already they were moving in on the International and taking away jobs Frank and his crew had been doing for years.

Frank was puzzled. In the first place he knew these guys who worked for him. He knew they drank and caroused. But he also knew they had pride in the International and would never intentionally or even accidentally mess up a job.

He and Czech had a long talk about it and Czech talked to each member of the crew to see if there was any chance they had messed up a job while in a hurry to get to a 3.2 break. Most of the guys were incensed at the very suggestion that they would mess up a job and cause Frank the Boss a problem. It was a mystery, and something had to be done. Czech also reminded the crew to be a little more careful with the squeegees, since they were going through the rubber inserts at a much faster pace than he could ever remember. The rubber inserts were the part that actually pulled the water off the window. They would wear out eventually but only left streaks if someone got careless and ran them over a piece of broken window, or a metal strip on the side of the window.

Everyone knew better than to do that yet that was apparently what was happening. The rubbers were coming in with cuts on them and would then have to be replaced.

That day everyone picked up their job slips and went out the door with long faces and questions in their minds about what Frank would do next.

Chippewa Charlie and Black Bill were the first ones in the door the next morning and when Czech walked in they both started talking at once. He hauled them up short and told them to start over one at a time.

Black Bill jumped in and told the story first.

Seems he and Chippewa Charlie had been hitting a few of the downtown joints the night before. They saw the Perfect Window Cleaning Truck pull up to a small store whose windows Charlie and Bill had cleaned earlier that same afternoon.

Now, long after the downtown stores were closed and with no one around to see them, the two owners of the Perfect Window Cleaning Company got out of the truck and proceeded to clean the already clean windows. Only they left long streaks down the center, and left muddy, dirty water all over the sidewalks under the windows.

The newcomers apparently followed the crews of the International and found out which jobs they did during the afternoon. They then went back at night to mess up the job.

As the rest of the crew members trickled in the story was repeated over and over. Chippewa Charlie and Black Bill taking turn explaining each detail. Czech added comments which turned the air blue in the immediate vicinity every time they began the story for a late arrival.

Frank the Boss got a big smile on his face when he heard Black Bill go through the report for the umpteenth time.

Instead of getting angry and upset like the rest of the crew, he seemed to be relieved that his crew was just as it had always been and the problem was from the outsiders.

He said he would visit the Perfect Window Cleaners, and make sure they contacted the businesses that had turned away from the International and let them know the true story.

The rest of the crew wasn't going to let it go quite that easy. Their integrity had been impugned. Though they were denizens of the skid and not high mucky mucks, they had their pride.

The morning bull session turned into a loud free for all of suggestions about how to take care of the scheming owners of the Perfect Window Cleaning Company.

The action when it came was unexpected. No one ever admitted to being the perpetrator. But it stopped the Perfect Window Cleaners as nothing else could have. As the crew of The International left the shop that morning for the day's run, one of the crew members, and no one ever found out which one, slipped out with a gallon of HyDee. Hydrochloric acid. During the day they searched out the truck driven by the Perfect Window Cleaners.

When they found it on a downtown street they pulled over with their truck and took care of the problem.

The Perfect Window Cleaning company owners were in a restaurant having their mid-morning coffee break.

The unknown crew members of the International emptied the entire gallon of HyDee into the two buckets of water sitting in the back of the competitor's pickup truck.

They followed and were on hand when the competitor's pulled up to their first job after the coffee break. Each of the Perfect Window Cleaners jumped out of the truck and grabbed their buckets, setting them on the sidewalk under the plate glass store windows. When they dipped their hands into the buckets to pick up a brush and sponge they jerked them out screaming in pain. Although they reacted quickly to the presence of the hydrochloric acid in the water it was not fast enough. A thousand fires were burning on each hand as the acid did its work. They pulled them out so quickly they sprayed the acid laced water all over themselves and their clothing.

By the time the ambulance arrived they were both in agony from the acid which was burning their clothes and skin. Their pants legs were hanging in shreds where the acid had burned through the cloth and onto their legs.

Months would pass before the acid burns would heal and by the time the healing took place the two out of towners had long since gone back to where they came from. They had learned a lesson they should have known. When you're taking on people who are used to taking care of themselves, people who live just a few blocks below the line where the city law ends and the street law begins, and when you threaten their already tenuous existence with dirty tricks, you had better be prepared to face the consequences.

Frank the Boss went through the motions of asking who could have done such a thing. You could tell he didn't have his heart in it. He knew his crew members well and he knew the answer before he asked the question.

No one else on the crew ever asked who had done it, preferring to be sincere in their ignorance in case the law ever did come around asking questions about the incident.

No one mentioned it again. Preferring to let the secret remain just that.

Czech found out the Perfect Window Cleaners had also been using a razor blade to slash the rubbers on the squeegees of International crew members. When they saw one unattended in a bucket they would make a small cut in the rubber which would then leave a streak on the glass and would have to be replaced. It was a dirty way to get jobs. Their stay in the Twin Cities ended quickly but the job pirates paid for a long time with every twinge of the burns on their arms and legs.

Chapter Twenty One - Preacher Roy

In war, there are no unwounded people. José Narosky

A reporter from South Dakota asked about the long haired protesters who were picketing in front of the White House. The leader of the free world talked about trying harder to understand the differences between the various groups who visited Washington. He said, "we have to try harder to be non-judgmental about those whose way of life differed from ours."

Being non-judgmental, and understanding the differences of the various crew members was a lesson everyone learned quickly at the International.

When your life depended on trusting the person you worked a building with, it mattered little what color their skin, how long their hair or how heavy their accent.

We were all from different backgrounds. The one thing most had in common was a need to find a bar or a bottle as soon after work as possible.

They seemed to bring whatever they were running away from with them as they moved into their new world on the skid.

The men I thought of as the homeless of the 50's were different in some ways from the homeless of later years, but the need for a bottle seemed to be the common denominator of those I knew in the fifties and those who called the steam grates of big city sidewalks home in later years.

Some came from the right side of the tracks and had known all manner of creature comforts. Others were born to the skid and had never known another life.

Preacher Roy was one member of the International crew who had come from a good family, from a well to do home, on the right side of the tracks.

Preacher came to us during the spring of the year as building owners began the spring cleaning chores and Frank was looking for more men to handle the added work load. Despite his idiosyncrasies Preacher seemed to fit right in at the International. Maybe it was because of those idiosyncrasies and not in spite of them.

He was tall and wore old, loose fitting clothes. Clothes that despite fading and wear, spoke of a better time in a different life. He looked like he had been sort of chubby at one time but life on the skid had thinned him down some. He lived in a flop house somewhere in the neighborhood of Washington and Hennepin in downtown Minneapolis. Harry the Cat said he had seen Preacher doing his panhandling in that area.

Harry would know since panhandling was his specialty and he knew who and where his competition was at all times.

The International had never had a window cleaner like Preacher Roy. Never anyone with so much education. It put some of the crew off a bit when the big man would start talking in Latin or Greek.

His name was Roy. We called him Preacher because of the Latin and Greek stuff. He had apparently grown up in a well-to-do home. He had gone to good schools and entered a seminary. It appeared from the little things he said that he had made it almost through the seminary when something happened that caused him to drop out, or caused the school to throw him out. No one knew for sure, and Preacher didn't talk about it.

He had a strange and unusual ability to raise his voice into a high falsetto and project it over quite a distance. The voice was like a keening whisper. It seemed to float to you from wherever he was working. Despite being very soft, barely above the volume of a whisper, it would carry a long way.

I still wonder how he did that.

It was like a ventriloquist throwing his voice.

He never seemed to move his lips. At least we couldn't see them move, and he never seemed to take a breath. The high, soft, whispering voice seemed to have no beginning and no end, it would just go on and on. You could be working on a ladder on the second floor of a downtown building, and suddenly amid the noise of traffic and the rumbling of streetcars this high, soft sound would be coming to you and around you. It really seemed to be coming from all around so it was hard to pinpoint the source.

The disembodied voice would likely as not be reciting the words of the wedding ceremony. "Dearly beloved, we are gathered here today to unite this man and this woman in holy matrimony."

On and on it would go through the entire wedding ceremony, picking up a rhythm as it went and never missing a word. All of the inflections and the emphasis would be placed in exactly the right places so you knew he had done this many times before.

Passersby would pause, look around, and try to figure out where this strange wedding was taking place, and seeing only a couple of window cleaners at work and no one else, would glance nervously around and then hurry on. Preacher had a strange sense of humor. He played practical jokes. His favorite seemed to be the wedding. The day would begin innocently enough, with the usual two or three man crew getting into a truck and heading out to a job. Often the job would be at a downtown building, and eventually the crew would be working the first and second floors.

One person would be on the ladder for the second floor, the other would be cleaning first floor windows.

Preacher usually volunteered for the ladder job. It was at this point that he would begin the wedding ceremony.

Passersby would look around and listen intently. Everyone on the crew knew what was coming. The further into the ceremony he got, the more nervous his working partner would become.

With that high falsetto voice drifting through the air in its soft keening whisper he would take this imaginary couple through the ceremony. Finally, at the climactic moment, he would intone, "do you Herring Choker take this woman to be your lawfully wedded wife?"

He would even answer "I do" for me or whichever coworker had been sent out to work with him that day.

Then came Preacher's big moment. He would slowly turn toward his coworker and ask, "Do you," and at this point he would insert the name of one of the prostitutes working that particular corner, "take Herring Choker to be your lawfully wedded husband?"

Again answering in the stead of the missing bride he would marry off his coworker to a neighborhood hooker.

It was weird, but the enjoyment he got from the wedding was obvious. It sounded for all the world like the real thing, and except for the lack of music, could have been an actual wedding taking place on the downtown Twin City streets.

Some of the guys got a little irritated when they heard themselves being wedded to one of the well-known street walkers who worked the avenue but most took it with a grain of salt and a little chuckle.

Until Czech got caught in the wedding trap that is.

It was a hot summer day. Czech didn't take well to the heat and humidity. And he took offense at even the suggestion that he, Czech, would have anything to do with a prostitute, much less be entered into holy matrimony with one.

He decked Preacher.

Oh, it was only one punch but it did send Preacher crashing to the sidewalk. He didn't hit him hard enough to cause any real damage but it caused enough ruckus that the store owner called the police.

By the time Frank arrived, the police had it sorted out.

Preacher met that night with Frank in his office, and didn't do the wedding thing again. Well at least not when Czech was around.

One day he was 10 or 12 feet up in the air working on the glass in a transom over a doorway and was amusing himself by performing some sort of religious rite in Latin while he worked.

He seemed to take a perverse pleasure in reciting all the religious stuff that was not supposed to be bandied about outside the sanctuary. On this particular day, as he gave his recitation in Latin, a distinguished looking member of the clergy walked out of the door just below where he was working. The elderly man of the cloth immediately began looking around for the source of this strange religious recitation. He looked first in the windows of the store and then went to the curb to look in the window of a parked car to see if the radio was on.

He finally pinpointed the source of the Latin incantation as being this strange looking window cleaner on top of the ladder.

"You there," the well-dressed clergyman called out in a commanding voice, "come down here."

Down came Preacher, looking somewhat crestfallen, as if he had been caught doing something he knew he shouldn't be doing, and of course he probably had been. "Where did you learn that son?" asked the clergyman in a much softer voice.

Preacher mumbled something audible only to the two of them. He said something about the seminary. The old cleric asked why he hadn't taken up the vocation and why was he here on the streets of the city. Preacher told the elderly cleric he didn't want to talk about it. He sort of hung his head and shuffled his feet around on the dirty sidewalk. The old man pressed him but couldn't get any answers. Finally placing a hand on Preacher's shoulder he said, "I'll pray for you son and if you ever need someone, if you ever want to talk about this, just call me and I'll come." The old cleric gave Preacher a card with his name and phone number on it and with a sad look climbed into his car and drove away.

Preacher put down the brush and squee-gee and headed for a 3.2 joint on the corner. Sometimes memories hurt so much they just can't be held back, I suppose that's the way it was with Preacher. He had gone to the right schools and apparently felt the call to the service of the church, but along the way something happened that was so bad he couldn't face the problem or his family. He had turned to the skid, where you never really had to face anything except the question of how to find enough money to pay for a jug of cheap wine and the two bit flop and slop for the night. We all wondered what had happened to him to make him step across the line to the other world, and begin his trek downward toward skid row, but we didn't get any answers then. They came only after many months had passed.

Chapter Twenty Two
Gorgeous George and His Prostitute Mother

*Each day of our lives we make deposits
in the memory banks of our children. Charles R. Swindoll*

It was quitting time on a late summer day when Loretta stopped by the International. No one had to ask who she was since many of the crew knew her already and those who hadn't met her had heard about her from the others. She was George's Mother.

With tinted red hair, the reddest rouge, lipstick, and plenty of Woolworth's cheapest cologne and powder, she was a caricature of a woman of the street.

It was obvious that George wished he was anywhere but there to greet his Mother. She was in a bad way. Closing in on fifty, and looking more like seventy, reeking of cheap whiskey, and obviously carrying a heavy burden on her booze-baffled mind, she leaned in the front door and called out in a hoarse voice, "George, George, I need you!"

Everybody sort of froze, and tried not to look at her or at her son who was heading for the front at a fast pace. That's when she lost her balance, fell through the door, and landed on the floor part way inside.

Half lifting and half dragging he managed to get her back outside, while asking, "What are you doing here? What do you want? You are not supposed to come here."

Her answer was muffled both by distance and by sobs which could have been from relief or remorse.

George moved her toward the corner, and disappeared down the street, leaving his tools on the back of the truck instead of cleaned and in the rack. Black Bill brought them in and cleaned them along with his and wondered out loud what Loretta's problem was.

George was unusually quiet the next morning, and didn't respond to the good natured ribbing and bantering which was standard morning fare in the bull session. His face looked even more haggard than usual as he went about the job of gathering up his tools and job slips for the day.

At noon while the rest of the crew headed for a sandwich or a 3.2 beer break, George disappeared, and was an hour late getting back on the job. That was all right. Ooftuh, Black Bill and Blind Bob and I did a few extra windows to cover him. When the others kidded him about being late he told them to back off that he had gone to take care of a problem.

Without his saying it, they knew who the problem was, but not what it was. When Blind Bob asked if he needed to take a couple of days, George agreed that he could use a couple days off to take care of the problem.

Bob finally came right out and asked. "Look George, if you've got a problem with your mother, you know the whole crew will help out. Now what's the problem?"

"She's in the hospital." George snarled, "She's gone and caught the syph and she's in the hospital, now are ya happy?"

Syphilis!

Everyone looked up at that one. That's the unspeakable disease that nobody wants around. It's what someone else gets, not your mother.

No wonder George was upset, everyone on the street knew it before him. The word travels fast in this kind of neighborhood, and the word was out.

Not only was she sick and in the hospital, but her working days in this neighborhood were over. In her profession this was like the kiss of death. No wonder she was boozed out of her mind the day she came to the shop. She had big troubles, and her medical condition was only one of them. She had a problem and had come looking for her son, probably for the first time in his life.

Now George had a problem. She needed a place to live and someone to take care of her when she was released from the hospital after the treatment with penicillin, which was the prescribed treatment of the day. Ultimately she would need some kind of a job to get her by until the street talk had faded and she could resume her profession.

George had a problem, and it was sort of a public problem, since so many of the guys knew his mother professionally.

That night Preacher waited until nearly everyone had gone and then invited George out for a beer. Although George had never been known to turn down a free beer, he said he had things to do and didn't have time.

Preacher was insistent and with only a little more urging than usual, convinced George that he really needed a quick one.

They went alone and no one knew for sure what transpired, but apparently Preacher's training hadn't been for naught.

The call to the service of the church, the call to reach out to people in need had been stronger than the pull of cheap wine and sleazy flea bag hotels. While pouring down a couple of beers, Preacher said, "George what your Mom really needs is a visit from a preacher.

It was doubtful that George had ever had a thought of religion in his entire life.

Even all those times on Sally's Soup line listening to the Salvation Army spiel it was doubtful that a thought of religion being a comfort to someone ever crossed his mind. Religion? A solace to someone on the far side of lonesome? Nothing like that had ever occurred to George.

He was the tough kid who grew up on the skid, on the take, living by his wits. Stealing, scamming, cheating, these were normal thoughts for someone of George's background.

Now here was a fellow denizen of the skid, suggesting that his Mother needed a prayer more than a shot of cheap booze.

By the time the barmaid had visited the booth several times, the dinner hour had passed and the county hospital visiting hours had arrived.

Filled with feelings of righteousness and fortified with plenty of liquid courage the son and the preacher made their way to the room of the errant lady of the night.

Arriving at the ward she was sharing with several other women, Preacher stepped to her bedside and with what passed for an air of solemnity and goodness, reached out to take her hand while muttering a half remembered Latin recitation.

Loretta turned the air blue with the language of the streets she knew so well. George quickly learned that Mom knew all about the Preacher and didn't need the last rites or anything else he had to offer.

The sheer volume of her response brought orderlies on the run and sent Preacher, his Latin platitudes and son George back out to the street where they promptly found a 3.2 joint to help them forget that awful encounter with Mama. George looked bad the next morning, and Preacher looked sad, sober, and distracted to the point that he had to be told a couple of times where his job slips would take him that day.

The encounter with George's Mother seemed to have had an effect on him that those working with him couldn't understand.

He stayed deep in thought for most of the next couple of days, and even turned down a chance to take a walking tour of the loop's hot spots with Black Bill and Chippewa Charlie.

Preacher showed up for work carrying a duffel bag one morning soon after the aborted good will visit to the hospital. At quitting time he grabbed the bag and headed for the shop's dark and little used shower room. Twenty minutes later he appeared, with hair slicked down with Wildroot cream oil, and sporting what appeared to be a well-worn sport coat and dress trousers, neither of which had apparently seen a cleaners for some time.

Frank the Boss called over to him, "They're here Roy, you better get a move on." Sure enough, a late model Ford Crestliner had pulled up in front of the shop and stopped.

The distinguished looking gray haired clergyman who had stopped him in the middle of his Latin liturgy months before stepped from the car and greeted Preacher with a warmth and kindness that he obviously hadn't experienced in a long time.

As they drove away, everyone turned to Frank the Boss who was standing by the window watching them go.

Turning from the window, he paused when he saw the entire crew staring and said, "You'll have to do without Roy for a few days' boys, I think he may have a new job. He's going to a meeting this afternoon and will let us know after that what's going to happen."

When nobody moved, and everyone sort of waited for something more, the boss man stepped out of his office and into the shop.

"Look guys," he said, "You know Roy Johnson, or Preacher, as you call him was a seminary student until something happened that made him quit when he was almost through the school. When he visited George's mother the other night it didn't come out too well, but he apparently found that he still wanted to be involved. He just couldn't be a preacher. He called the Reverend over at the church and talked to him about a plan he had worked out to start a street ministry in the skid row area he knows so well.

He told the church people about George's mother and all the others like her who lived on the skid, and who had no way out when they had a problem. He talked to them about some of the things they could do and the various ways they could offer a helping hand."

As we found out later, someone else had tried to start a program similar to that a couple of years earlier, but had dropped it when they couldn't get a response from the women they were trying to reach. Now with Preacher working with them, they figured they had found the way.

"Apparently," said Frank, "they feel Roy can be a big part of their ministry, and may be able to finish his school and get ordained or whatever it is those people need to do. Preacher just might have found what he's been looking for, if so, he won't be back."

The crew of The International was quiet, as if they couldn't quite see how this big man they had worked with and caroused with, could now minister to the women on the skid. Yet glad that he was going to get his chance in the real world, and proud that they might have helped him on his way.

There were a lot of people who moved through the crew of the International. For some the company provided the half way stop on their way off the skid and out of their nightmare.

For others it became a wayside on the way down. A place where they could rest a bit and maybe try and find an answer to whatever was troubling them. Failing that, they would consign themselves to a life of panhandling enough each day for a jug of wine and a flop and slop for the night.

Each of them seemed to have an effect on the others as they came and went. Some, like Preacher, made the turn and started the climb back out of their personal hell and stopped by from time to time to share their good luck with the others.

It was never the same though. Once they had started the climb, no matter how close they had been during their stay at the International, when they came back to visit, it was different.

They talked and laughed together, but a strain was there, a feeling that the visitor was no longer one of them, but was instead, somehow connected, now, with the high mucky mucks. The folks who laid down rules the rest of us had to live under. As if they had stepped over a line into a different dimension and just didn't quite fit in any more.

There was tension in the air when Preacher tried to talk with his former crew members. He was the reformed. The goodness and worth whileness of his life made their existence all the more drab and their lives seem all the more unimportant. It was like they felt a sense of shame because he knew where they were heading after work and even though he had been there many times with them, deep down they knew there was another life, if only they could make the choice. But of course, they couldn't.

Chapter Twenty Three - Preacher Roy Comes Home

Failure doesn't mean you are a failure
it just means you haven't succeeded yet. Robert Schuller

Fall had come and the first snifters of dirty gray snow had begun drifting into the alleys and between the cracks of the broken sidewalks of the city the morning Preacher came home. He didn't just walk in for a visit as he had been doing, quite often since he left to work on his Skid Row Mission.

This time Czech found him passed out in the doorway of the International early on a cold and frosty morning.

He was sleeping off a drunk like any derelict on the skid.

Czech hauled him inside out of the cold and made a pot of coffee, while the rest of the crew drifted in for the day.

You could see Frank the Boss take a deep breath and see his jaw tighten up just a bit when he saw Preacher stretched out by the stove obviously suffering the effects of a binge that had been going on for some time.

"What's the story Czech?" He asked in a voice that sounded angry, sad, and unbelieving all at once.

"I don't know Frank," Czech replied, with a shake of his head, "He's been out like a light since I found him passed out in the doorway. "He was half froze. It was only 18 degrees out there this morning and he must have been there half the night."

"Well," Frank said, to no one in particular, "at least he knew where to come. Why don't you and Joe take one of the trucks and haul him down to Lil's, she'll know what to do with him."

So Preacher was back, and everyone was wondering what went wrong. He had started the climb out of the skid and after nearly a year it looked like he had made it.

He visited often enough and looked so good no one saw it coming. But like others on the skid, he could hide his problems and scam everyone around, including the authorities who it seemed, forever hassled you when you were down.

"Well," Joe said, "He made the good try, and perhaps he will try again when the grand lady Miss Lilly has made him better." Everyone knew that Miss Lilly of the Palace Hotel could work wonders on "Frank's boys" and would treat them with kindness and dignity when he sent them down for the treatment. Sure enough, the next morning Preacher showed up, looking crestfallen, morose, and shifty eyed, as if he felt a deep shame for having let everyone down.

"You ready to clean some windows Skinner?" asked Czech, as he got out a new bucket and some tools.

"Yeah, Yeah I'm ready," Preacher replied in a low voice no one else could hear, "And this time I'm back for good."

No one questioned it, and we all started loading up our gear, but with great reluctance. Obviously everyone wanted to be there to hear the story. It wasn't forthcoming so the crew finally headed out for the day.

As days turned into weeks, we all wondered, what had happened to cause his fall from grace. Preacher didn't volunteer anything so his return was about the same as when one of the others disappeared for a few days on a drunk and then turned up in the doorway ready to go back to work. Only this was different. Preacher had taken a big step. He had moved back into a real life in the real world, and had fallen off the wagon, back into the old life in the "other" world.

Everyone wondered why.

When the story broke, it broke in a big way. Like nothing that had ever happened to anyone at the International.

It was Mexican Joe who came in one morning and asked Frank the Boss if he could talk to him in his office. He could be seen giving a magazine to Frank, who sat down, shook his head, and started to read.

Joe had discovered a national magazine with a big picture of Preacher inside, and with it a story about the work he was doing with his skid row ministry.

It was Preacher all right, being praised by many of the citys high mucky mucks for the good he was doing. The writer even suggesting that this program could be duplicated on a larger scale all over the country.

It was the story and the notoriety it brought with it that was Preacher's undoing. The rest of the story unfolded slowly in the weeks to come.

First though Frank the Boss called Preacher into his cubby hole office and asked him if there was a problem that he could help with. He sort of thought, like some of the rest, that maybe preacher was trying to hide from the law or the authorities and when the story hit he felt he had to run, but that wasn't it.   Preacher told Frank that a lady from a small paper in White Bear Lake had heard about the Skid Row Mission and had called for an interview for a story in their limited circulation weekly.

Although Preacher resisted and said press coverage would have a bad effect on the program, the board of directors of the church group thought a story might bring in some donations that would help keep it going.

Preacher finally agreed, and the writer snapped a picture of him to go with the story. The picture was the problem. After the weekly paper had used the story the ambitious writer thought it deserved wider circulation and sent it off to a couple of magazines, to make an extra buck and to get some big time national exposure for herself and the organization.

To Preacher's chagrin, the story was accepted, published, and gave him the exposure he had avoided.

The call from his Mother came within a few days of the story's publication; it apparently wasn't a happy call.

"Your Father," she told Preacher, "is in the hospital and doesn't have long to live. The only thing he wants is to see you before he goes."

Preacher, heeding his mother's pleas had gone back home to visit his father in the hospital. When the tearful visit was completed he had gone directly from the hospital to the nearest tavern and couldn't remember where he had gone from there, or for that matter, how he had reached the doorway of the International.

Everyone had wondered what happened to Preacher that took him out of a good home, into the seminary, and then onto the skid rows of America. They weren't going to find out now either. That was as much as Preacher would tell.

He did stay out of the bars though and didn't take part in the afterhours carousing of the rest of the crew. He seemed sad and withdrawn.

That didn't affect his work though. Preacher Roy knew how to clean windows. If you drew him for a partner on a building job you knew he would more than carry his end of the load.

Three months passed and on a below zero mid-winter St. Paul afternoon his Mother showed up at the International. The car she was in was a top of the line silver grey Caddy. The broad shouldered muscular guy behind the wheel looked as much like a body guard as he did a chauffeur.

You could see she was one of the high mucky mucks and looked around with distaste as she made her way across the cracked and dirty sidewalk to the door which Frank the Boss hurried over to open.

The voice was patrician, and filled with a certain ring of authority as she introduced herself to Frank and said she would like to have a word with him in private.

He glanced at the small messy room which he called his office, shrugged his shoulders, and invited her in for what turned out to be a long meeting.

Black Bill came in later, carrying two buckets and two safety belts and for once seemed at a loss for words.

"Preacher and I were coming in from the job" he said, "and as we came around the corner, he saw the Caddy parked in front of the International. He dropped his bucket and belt and took off toward downtown."

When Frank saw Bill arrive he stuck his head out of the office door and said "Bill, where's Roy?"

Bill gave his report on the fast disappearing Preacher one more time for Frank, and backed away fast as the fine lady in the office burst into tears.

"He's gone," she cried softly, "He's gone and we'll never find him again. This time he's gone for good."

Frank closed the door and listened without a word as the story of Preacher was finally explained.

"It started," she said, "in late 1942 when Roy," her oldest son, "graduated from high school. It was my fault. It was all my fault."

Like every other 18 year old coming out of high school during World War Two, Roy was ready to head off to an army boot camp and then in 10 or 12 weeks it was off to the European or Pacific Theaters of Operation as the two major battle fronts of the War were called.

"Roy was ready," she said," and he talked at length with his father about the war and the army and everything."

Roy's mother however, had other ideas. And after days of arguing convinced him that the war would be over in a few months and that nothing would be gained by his getting involved at this late date.

"For my sake." she said, "you should enter the seminary as you have talked about and as a means of avoiding the draft."

He had talked about the seminary but had never made the commitment.

She told Frank it was with great reluctance and only after she cried and told him he owed it to her and to his Father to avoid the draft that he finally agreed to her plan and entered the seminary.

The story got around town fast. With Gold Star Flags going up in windows all over town telling the community of another son killed in battle, Roy the draft dodger was about the lowest form of life around. His 17-year old brother took the flak. But only for a couple of weeks. "Then," Roy's mother said, "he ran away from home, lied about his age, faked his father's signature and joined the Marines." They had no idea where he was until he turned 18 and was old enough to be in the service. A year passed and when they saw the Marine officer at the door, they didn't have to guess why he was there. He handed them the telegram informing them that their youngest son had been killed in action on an island in the Pacific.

They drove to the seminary to break the news to Roy. She said, "Roy's grief was a terrible thing to see."

"It should have been me" he kept saying, "It should have been me. If I had gone he would never have run away. He wouldn't have been there. It should have been me."

"He was still repeating it over and over," she said, as he walked out of the seminary and out of their lives.

Roy fled the seminary and disappeared. He remained out of sight and out of communication until the magazine article brought him back.

After Roy talked to his father in the hospital, the horror of his brother's death returned in full force and still unable to face that terrible memory, he disappeared again.

"This time," she told Frank, "I was able to track him down through the people at the skid row mission who told her about the International."

The story was long and nearly two hours had passed before the weeping woman finished. Despite Frank's reassurances that her son would be found she still shook her head saying, "No, I have lost them both. By trying to hang on to them my sons are both gone and it's my fault. It's all my fault."

The crew had cleaned their tools and stowed them away for the night. Most lingered as long as possible to hear the outcome of the visit but as it continued on most finally left for the Pigs Eye.

The darkness of mid-winter descended on the office. Lights were turned on and still she stayed, sharing with Frank a story that had been bottled up inside for all the years since the war.

It was just after six when Frank heard the outer door open and turned to see the old preacher who had befriended Roy and brought him into the Skid Row Ministry.

Preacher Roy, with head down and eyes averted followed him through the door.

"Roy" his Mother gasped, "Roy, I thought you were gone, I thought I would never see you again."

The old minister nodded his head at Frank who took the hint and rising said, "We're going to leave you two alone while you get things sorted out."

"Roy, I'm so sorry, I am so sorry," his mother was saying as Frank and The minister left the room.

The next day Preacher was gone back to his Skid Row Mission for fallen women. He had finally faced his brother's death and the nightmare that had haunted him every waking hour for all the years since the war.

Everyone nodded their heads the next morning when Mexican Joe said, "Now the Preacher man has found himself. Before he couldn't look inside because he hated what he saw; now he can look inside and remember his little brother in a different way, a better way."

Joe was usually right about stuff like that and we all agreed he probably had this one figured right too.

Maybe Preacher won't ever like himself because of what he did, but as his mother said, it was her fault, not his.

Doesn't seem right, does it, that one man like Hitler could exact this terrible toll on the lives of so many millions of people, not just during the war, but for all of those years and years afterwards.

For some the war is over. For others it just keeps on hurting and for many the pain never ends. It manifests itself in as many ways as there are men and women who carry it in their memory.

For some the painful memories become the spur that carries them to success as they try to make sure no one else will ever have to face what they have faced. For others it's the grease on the slide down toward the skid row streets of the America.

Unlike Preacher, most of their stories never get told. The memories remain bottled up in the hearts and minds of this lost generation.

Those fear filled memories fill their entire being as they try desperately to escape them in the solitude of a skid row flop and slop or the neon lit, smoke filled back booth of a Pig's Eye Saloon.

Preacher will always carry in his heart and mind, the pain of his brother's death, but maybe now it will ease enough to allow him to rejoin the real world, and he will never again have to face the prospect of passing out in the doorway of the International on an 18 degree Minnesota winter morning.

Chapter Twenty Four - Bottle Bill

If the misery of the poor be caused not by the laws of nature but by our institutions, great is our sin. Charles Darwin

The president was asked questions about the homeless people living on the streets and the ever increasing distance between the haves and the have not's in America.

I thought again of the window cleaners of the International. Some of them were the homeless of the 50's, only the term homeless hadn't come into vogue yet. In the early fifties, they were still being referred to as skid row bums, derelicts, hobos and panhandlers. The dregs of humanity in that fast moving society of the post war years.

Many were homeless, to the extent that they had no permanent address, and for the most part, had learned to live within the system that kept them on the street, living a hand to mouth existence in the familiar flop and slop bed and breakfasts of the skid row neighborhoods.

Bottle Bill was one of these old time skid row bums. He could carry a whiskey flask, tucked tightly up under his arm, while he cleaned windows all day and would never spill a drop.

He got his nick name when the State Legislature was considering one of those bottle deposit laws and referred to it as a "Bottle Bill". Somebody on the crew suggested that he go over to the Legislature and testify since he had more experience depositing bottles than anybody around.

He managed to get out of sight periodically during the day to lighten the weight of his bottle a little, or perhaps it was just a transfer of the weight from the bottle to his stomach. By days end it was usually light enough that I think any of us could have carried it under our arm.

Bottle Bill always volunteered to be on the crew that cleaned the windows on the North Side Liquor Distributor Warehouse, and would work outside until the water in his bucket was real dirty, before heading inside to work in the warehouse area.

He always managed to slip three or four bottles of what he referred to as "inventory," into his bucket, before he finished the job. Hidden by sponge, brush, squeegees and the dirty water, the whiskey would safely reside in his bucket until we got a couple of blocks away from the warehouse.

Bill would then say, "Pull over for a minute while I dump my water and clean up my tools." He would disappear then. We knew we wouldn't see Bill until his "inventory" was gone.

Bill thought cleaning the windows at the whiskey warehouse was like having Christmas four times a year, which was how often we went there.

He had spent a lot of time on the skid rows of America, and told stories about the people he had met along the way. He made them sound like real people. People, like him, who had once lived and worked in the real world. For some reason they had drifted onto the skid, and once there, they stayed on the skid, comfortable with their panhandling routes, and well known by the people they mooched along the way.

The reasons they gave for being on the skid were numerous. Booze seemed to be the substance they used to grease the slide for the trip down but it was usually something else that got them started on the sauce.

An abusive home life, a false hearted love, a failed business, the excuses were many. They blamed their slide down from the real world and into the "other world," as most of them called their life on the skid, on someone else. It was never their fault.

According to Bottle Bill, there was a new generation of people moving onto the skid rows of America in the fifties, and these newcomers would, as he put it, "slit your throat for your socks." He said it wasn't like the good old days before the war when you could live on the skid and not worry about those you shared the flop houses with at night. Since the war years, he thought a new breed who cared less for others, and were less likely to help each other were taking over the areas of town which had been home to him and his friends.

Even so, he seemed to face life with an attitude that said, "You've hit me with everything you've got, and I took it, so you don't worry me none."

Thin from all those years of never quite enough greasy-spoon-restaurant food, and with a face lined from the booze, cigarettes, and the nights spent on the street with nowhere to sleep, he still managed to maintain an attitude.

Not a bad attitude, not a good attitude, just an attitude.

You knew where you stood with Bill. You never got too close.

The day he came to work with a worried look about him, obvious enough so that most of us noticed it, changed that.

When a guy who never seemed to worry about anything except where the next two bit flop and slop was coming from, wore a worried look, you just had to notice. Flop and slop was what he called the twenty five cents a night skid row bed and breakfast emporiums.

Blind Bob was working with him that day on the Three M, the new Minnesota Mining and Manufacturing Buildings on the East side, and had a chance to visit with him.

That wasn't easy because Bottle Bill didn't really like people asking questions or taking up time with talk that didn't mean anything. He wasn't much for visiting.

When he wouldn't respond to anything else Bob finally asked straight out "Bill, what's gnawing on ya anyway?"

It took a while, but Bill finally let out that he might be in a little trouble with "Lucky's" boys.

Lucky being "The Man."

The local kingpin of punch cards, prostitutes, betting and gambling of just about any kind.

Bob said, "Bill how could you get mixed up with people like that, you've never had any money to gamble with?"

Seems Bill had found an envelope stuffed with money on the seat of a back booth at a bar. It was like Christmas in July and he blew the whole wad on a few nights out on the town.

Bad move.

It was part of the days punch card take for Lucky. His "boys" had left the envelope lying on the seat in the tavern booth while trying to pick up a stripper working the lounge. They were now in big trouble with the boss.

They checked around to find out who had been in the bar while they were otherwise occupied.

The word was out. They were on the prod looking for him.

It could have been rough for the old guy if they had actually caught up with him, even though it wasn't a lot of money, it was enough to make "The Boys" mad.

Of course you couldn't really blame them. They had to face Lucky himself and tell him they had lost some of his money while trying to pick up one of the strippers in this just-off-the- loop strip joint.

The barkeep said later they not only lost the cash, they struck out with the stripper too. They were mad.

When the rest of the crew heard about it they took up a collection, and a couple of the guys took their tools and went down on Robert Street where they picked up a few extra jobs and donated the money to Bottle Bill who then prepared to "donate" it back to Lucky's Boys. He really appreciated the help and looked for a minute like he was going to cry when the crew brought the envelope with the cash to him that morning. He was still worried though, about how to get the money back to Lucky's boys.

Bob said, "You know, I bet they wouldn't bother Clyde none, if he took it to them."

Clyde being the biggest man on the crew. His name wasn't really Clyde, but everyone called him that because he was so big they compared him to the Clydesdale work horses used to haul beer wagons in the TV ads, and in the state fair horse pulling contests every year at fair time.

Clyde decided he could do that and after Frank the Boss got everyone lined out for their day's work Clyde started hitting the downtown bars looking for "Lucky's Boys." He eventually found them in the same strip joint where they had lost the money.

By then Clyde had visited half the joints in downtown St. Paul, and had picked up plenty of "Jim Beam Courage," as he called it.

When the behemoth spotted The Boys, in their wide shouldered, sharply tapered "Zoot" suits he was fairly roaring. They offered no resistance when he told them a friend of his had found some of their money and wanted to return it.

He told the crew later, it was obvious they were surprised to get the money back, and equally obvious that they had no desire to be anything but respectful to the huge man who showed them their way back into Lucky's good graces.

Lucky and the boys were not people to tangle with, but then neither was Clyde. Especially when the rest of the crew had given him a free walking tour of St. Paul's finest drinking establishments, while pursuing such a noble goal.

Chapter Twenty Five - The Last Scam of Gorgeous George

Injustice is relatively easy to bear; it is justice that hurts. ~H.L. Mencken

Everyone who comes from the wrong side of the tracks doesn't develop the high standards, the work ethic, or the determination to succeed that Orbit had demonstrated for the crew of the International.

Gorgeous George was a product of skid row. A lifelong resident of the slums, he learned, early in life the art of the scam.

Whether it was Frank the Boss, another member of the crew, or the police, George could lay a scam on them with the best.

His earliest memories were of a prostitute mother sending him out into the hallway of the tenement they called home so she could go to work.

It was in these hallways and on these streets, littered with broken wine and whiskey bottles that he received his education. These streets which were fouled by the people who dwelled on them were his classrooms.

People who scooted into doorways when a stranger walked by and those who gathered in the alleyways to discuss new ways to get a buck for a bottle were his teachers. From them he learned to look the high mucky mucks in the eye and to mouth the words they wanted to hear.

Whether he was being hassled by the authorities or pulling a scam on someone new to the neighborhood, he learned that to look someone in the eye was the secret to gaining their trust. That if you listened carefully you would soon find out what it was they wanted to hear. You would say those words in a forthright and convincing way and you would be believed.

From them he learned that whenever you were caught by anyone in authority you should always have some little bit of information that could be useful to them. Information they could elicit from you by what they believed to be skillful questioning. If they got something from you, anything that could easily be proven true, they would likely be satisfied and question you no further. Gorgeous George had learned well the lessons the masters of the scam taught him.

So when Preacher Roy had gotten his mother off the street and into a vocational program and began to work on George, he knew all of the right answers. He knew the words to say that would give Roy the impression that he, too, was moving toward a straight life in the real world.

He moved adroitly between the various worlds he lived in. From the International, to the skid, to the vocational programs of Preacher, his words satisfied nearly everyone that he was trying to do things that would keep him out of the Pig's Eye saloon and lead him into a more productive life.

Most of the International crew members knew otherwise. They had scammed enough themselves to know which end was up. While friendly with George, they always held him at arm's length, knowing that if he got too close, or if you opened up too much, or relaxed too much, he would quickly take advantage.

So it was when George began flashing large bills at the Pig's Eye after work. When he disappeared during the day for an hour or so and came back with a grin and a pocketful of cash. We all knew something was coming down and at some point George would lay a scam on the wrong person and would pay for it. You always paid when you went for the easy buck.

It was easy to believe that he was working a scam, and equally easy to believe he would be caught, and that anyone close to him would be answering questions for a long time.

Preacher heard about the cash and the daily breaks from work. Having lived the life himself he knew this was building toward a bad day for George. He took him out for a beer and tried to talk to him about the problems that were going to come if he was into something illegal, which we were all certain he was.

Even Loretta, his mother, stopped him on the street and said, "George honey, I've heard the street talk about all the money you've been flashing. This doesn't sound good. Why don't you listen to Roy? He could help you."

George had answers. He knew what to say and how to say it.

It was Czech who stumbled on the answer to George's sudden wealth during a late night visit to the Pig's Eye. While heading for the back booth which was the usual haunt of the crew of the International he spotted George in the company of two of Lucky's boys.

They weren't hard to spot with their dark colored, sharply tailored "Zoot" suits and grey hats. They were sitting in a side booth and on the table were the familiar punch boards and betting slips which brought Lucky's financial empire much of its wealth.

So that was it. George had hooked on as a runner with Lucky's boys and was being used to transport illegal gambling paraphernalia around the downtown area. This would be right down his alley since he knew the back streets like the back of his hand.

Czech knew, and anyone who knew George knew, that he would never be satisfied with the money they paid him for being their gambling gopher in downtown St. Paul. We all knew that anytime George had a chance to scam someone he eventually would do just that. In his own good time he would try and skim some of Lucky's cash into his own pockets.

George was just that way and no amount of money in his pocket would keep him from trying for a little more. Only this time he was playing with the pros and would be in trouble big time if he made the wrong move.

The next morning Czech scheduled himself to work with George and during the mid-morning 3.2 break tried to explain just how rough Lucky's people could be if you tried the wrong move on them. He tried to warn him that he should get out of the business while he still had a chance.

He wasn't telling George anything he didn't already know. Even though the advice was unsolicited George told him he appreciated the thought and said he was planning to get out as soon as he had enough money to get a car and get into school so he could get off the skid once and for all.

Czech knew he was being scammed and George knew that Czech knew and he also knew that Czech was right, that a false move would bring the wrath and certain retribution of a man who had a reputation to uphold.

Loretta came to Frank for help and asked him if he would talk with her son. Frank did as she asked, knowing that little would come of his efforts.

There was an air of finality in the air whenever any of the crew talked about George. It was if everyone knew that he was going to end up on the wrong side of "the boys" and that it was only a matter of time.

George had never been a particularly popular member of the crew and had bullied and tricked most of us into taking the outside on big jobs on the coldest days of winter. He had taken advantage of everyone on the crew at one time or another.

Still, no one wanted anything serious to happen to him and trouble with the local hoods was as serious as it came.

It wasn't unusual for George, or any other member of the crew to disappear for a few days once in a while, so when George didn't show up for work for several days in a row no one was overly concerned.

The day a couple of "the suits" stopped Czech on the street was the first inkling that something had happened. They asked Czech about Georges' whereabouts. They wanted to know where he was working.

Czech said, "George hasn't been to work for several days."

The biggest suit wanted to know more about his hang outs and where he could usually be found.

Czech told them, knowing full well that George was long gone.

It was late summer when two detectives from St. Paul police came to the International looking for someone who knew George. They were trying to find a wife or other relative.

Frank told them about Loretta and where to find her and then asked what they knew about George.

The officer said, "They found him in an alley in Chicago on the south side of the loop under the El."

The Chicago police told them it wasn't pretty. George had been worked over by the pros who made sure he would be seen as an example.
They said, "Whatever he was into it was obvious he was meant to be found and the perpetrators wanted the world to know what had happened to him."

Chicago authorities wanted to know where to ship the body and whether there were any relatives who would accept responsibility for it.

For the crew of The International it was not a surprise and there was little sympathy for George.

Everyone felt bad for Loretta.

She had given George few of the things mothers normally give to their kids having spent the best years of her life standing on dimly lit street corners waiting for a john instead of at home with her son.

But she had turned over a new leaf and with the help of Preacher had turned her life around. She had tried to share this new start in life with George. Unfortunately, his ways were set. He was destined to play the hand he had been dealt, right up to the end.

It was a week before the body arrived at the county morgue and out of respect for Loretta the crew made the ritual trip to The Ridges for the burial.

Mexican Joe, as usual, found a few things to say that gave the moment whatever religious connotation the burial of a scam artist could muster up.

Preacher Roy joined in and whatever he said was obviously designed to help Loretta. No one else in the group had any way to help the departed or his mother. Everyone climbed into the company trucks and headed for the Pig's Eye. Even Preacher joined in as they "hoisted one to the memory of the dearly departed."

George wasn't really missed by anyone on the crew.

It was sort of like the saying, out of sight out of mind.

Born into a different lifestyle, George's gift for sizing up any situation he was in and saying the things people wanted to hear could have made him one of the high mucky mucks in town since many of them seem to have the gift as well.

But he wasn't born into a different world. He was born on the skid and during his brief sojourn on earth had led a strange, precarious and unique type of existence.

Unlike Orbit who overcame the problems of the life he had been born into, George had developed no standards that could make of him anything other than what he was.

Orbit through his own effort made the move up, while George started from the bottom and went down from there.

Maybe that's what the president meant when he talked about a lack of moral certainty in the lives of those without hope, those born into circumstances that prevented them from becoming part of what he called the American Dream.

But why do some, like Orbit, find that moral certainty and dare to reach out for the dream? It has to be more than their surroundings. It has to be something inside. Perhaps it was someone who touched them with a word, an idea or an ideal.

If the president, or any of the "inside the beltline crew" ever figures out the answer to that one they'll probably be made president for life.

Chapter Twenty Six - Mexican Joe And His American Dream

*If you take advantage of everything America has to offer,
there's nothing you can't accomplish. Geraldine Ferraro*

The President was answering questions about things the United States was doing to help third world countries bring a better standard of living to their peoples. He talked at length about the illegal immigration of Mexicans across the southern U.S. borders and the problems the nation faced in caring for them. He spoke of the problems the illegal immigrants faced as they tried to grab the brass ring and win for themselves a portion of the American Dream. Many, he said, faced nearly insurmountable problems with the language, with customs, and with the discrimination they faced as they tried to get jobs and provide for their families without the papers necessary to move into the real world.

He said, "It's an underworld where they could be taken advantage of and virtually enslaved by the unscrupulous who would profit from their misery.

There were some who did find their American Dream. Mexican Joe was one. No one ever asked and no one ever knew or cared whether he had the legal papers or not. Joe just went about doing his job and being a friend.

I often wondered if all Mexicans were as cheerful and happy go lucky as Joe. No matter what was going on around him he seemed to keep his same even tempered outlook on life.

People who occupied the offices in the buildings where we worked were always happy to see "Joe the Window Cleaner" coming. It didn't matter whether the office was occupied by file clerks or CEO's; they all reacted to his presence in pretty much the same way.

Joe was unique. I asked him once if everyone south of the border was as cheerful as he was. He shook his head saying, "No Mister Del, they are just like everyone else. Some are grumpy and some are happy. We each have to decide for ourselves which way we want to be."

He obviously had made his decision and tried every day to cheer up the rest of the world too.

His concern about others was obvious and people seemed to sense that he would show sympathy or compassion, which ever was appropriate, and many would go out of their way to tell him about some family problem they were dealing with.

It was late in February when one of the high mucky mucks in the Merchandise Mart told Joe his little girl was having severe health problems and doctors couldn't seem to find out what the trouble was.

He looked really worried and Joe listened with great attention, asking questions about eating snd sleeping habits, skin color and other symptoms.

The next day he skipped a morning coffee break and went back to the businessman's office with a box of herbs and told the businessman exactly how to treat his daughter with them, and where they all came from.

Joe had discussed the case with his mother who immediately began giving him instructions on how the condition would have been treated in the old country. She even had the herbs she had brought with her when Joe brought her to Minnesota from Mexico months before.

The startled businessman wasn't sure how to react when Joe presented him with the package of herbs but listened with growing interest as Joe related how many people his mother had helped in the old country with the same treatment.

Joe had aloe and showed the worried Father how to fix wild strawberries. The leaves to help fight the weakness his daughter felt and the berries to help her kidneys work properly. He had balsam root which he said would overcome scurvy and vitamin C to help the digestive tract and kidneys. There was bark for weakness and other herbs, each to help the sick girl's body heal itself.

Joe pointed out that we have strong bodies which will heal themselves naturally if we just help them along with the right amount of nutrients and drink lots of water to keep our systems working properly.

Joe's Mother thought the little girl had consumption, or at least that was as close a translation as Joe could offer the father who became increasingly interested in the variety of herbs leaves and berries Joe showed him.

He asked so many questions Joe finally looked at his watch and muttered something in Spanish before jumping up and reminding us that we had a full day's worth of windows to clean and were far behind schedule.

Weeks went by and one day Frank received a call from the business man asking about Joe's position with the company and about his family.

His daughter, he told Frank, was recovering slowly from whatever her health problem had been. He credited Joe and his mother for the recovery since several doctors had continued to be puzzled over the illness and suggested they didn't have a cure for her ailment.

"What can I do for Joe?" was the question he posed to Frank, "to show our appreciation."

Frank told him that Joe was unlikely to accept anything for his help, since helping people was just something he did.

It was as natural as breathing, according to Joe. Someone had a problem, and you did what you could to help them.

It didn't matter whether they were residents of skid row or high mucky mucks in ivory towers whose windows Joe cleaned.

The man was sure there was something he could do and asked Frank if he would send Joe over to his office where they could talk it over.

I have to say, he handled it really well.

"If you could have anything in the world, what would you want?" was the question he posed to Joe. "What one thing would help you and your family the most?"

Without a moment's hesitation Joe told him about his family's dream of owning a neighborhood Ma and Pa grocery store.

Today they would be called "convenience stores," but in those days, they were "Ma and Pa" neighborhood grocery stores and every family made several trips a week to the corner store for bread, eggs and milk.

"This is what our family will have someday," said Joe, "A neighborhood store where we will offer only the best vegetables which we will grow ourselves and even some of Mama's herbs for our neighbors and friends, to keep them strong, and we will name it after my Mother, Rosa."

"Mama Rosas' grocery," he said, "will help the people in our neighborhood, and help our children go to the university so they will be important people. They will help others with their work. This is what we dream, Mama and I, when we talk about what America has given us and how we can give something back to America by helping our neighbors."

It was a fine speech. One that perhaps should be heard by the people who complain about how tough things are now, and how they just can't get ahead, and how the country is going down the tubes.

A few days later the same businessman came by the shop during the evening bull session and asked Joe if he had time to go for a ride with him to take a look at a property he owned on the south side near Joe's home.

There, in what would be considered the poor side of town, or the other side of the tracks, on the south side of the city was a five acre plot of land with an old abandoned gas station garage on one corner.

"I've owned this land for several years" the businessman told Joe, and thought that someday we would plat it out and build apartments on it but this might be just the place for your store. You would have room for a vegetable garden in the back so you could raise vegetables and herbs to sell in the store."

He then set a price on the land and explained to Joe how he would carry the note while Joe got his business established. "You can pay for your store out of the profits," he said.

The price was low, the terms were certainly right and in a few short weeks, Joe the window cleaner became Joe the Southside businessman, proprietor of his own grocery store.

For once, Joe told us in the bull session the next morning, he couldn't say a word. The old long vacated garage would take a lot of remodeling but with Joe's large family there were lots of helping hands. They started the garden right away so there would be produce to sell by mid-summer.

"I'll feel my family is helping your family and all of the families in your neighborhood," the businessman said. He set up a prepaid account with a wholesale food distributor and said, "when the store is ready your first groceries are paid for."

It was an unlikely turn of events for a guy who had figured on saving for twenty years for the down payment on a lot much less five whole acres. Joe immediately began remodeling the old building and with his family helping soon had a gas station and grocery store opened. It was a big day for the family when they invited all of his co- workers to the Grand Opening.

As the International's crew talked about the new store word spread through the office buildings in downtown St. Paul where the cheerful window cleaner was so well known.

On the morning of the big day, workers from buildings all over St. Paul began arriving with flowers, garden tools, and presents of all kind for the bewildered Mexican family.

With "Mama Rosa" ensconced on a stool by the cash register, children filling grocery bags, and running errands, Joe greeting friends and his wife trying to keep things straight, none of them seemed to really understand what was happening.

The outpouring of gifts from people who knew him only through his visits to their offices stunned even Joe. He greeted each new arrival with a welcome and thank you in both English and Spanish.

For Joe, his family and for all of his neighbors who would be regular customers it was a day to remember. One that would make them feel good every time they thought about the high mucky mucks from the other world, from downtown, who came to their neighborhood to honor one of their own.

Joe kept on washing windows while the family ran the store, pumped gas and raised garden produce to sell.

When one of the crew asked Joe what made him so lucky, Joe just got a big smile on his face and explained how lucky we all were to be able to live and work in this great country.

Joe didn't have much formal education but he seemed to have more knowledge of people than most people with all their doctorates. His sense of fairness and honesty lifted him head and shoulders above most of us.

As he walked into the offices in the buildings in the city, he was greeted with even more enthusiasm.

Office workers seemed to feel a bond with the man they had honored with their gifts at his big grand opening day.

The American flag he wore above the white visor of his bus driver's hat seemed to take on new meaning. He showed us that the American Dream, even in the fifties, was very much a living dream. People who went through life with a fantastic attitude could expect fantastic results.

It's funny how many of us take what we have for granted. Someone who has never had this *good life,* as Joe called it, comes along and by appreciating everything they receive through their hard work get luckier and luckier.

As the saying goes, the harder I work, the luckier I get. That's the way it was with Joe and his family. He was always ready to extend a helping hand to anyone. Rich or poor, old or young, everyone was treated the same. Most people treated him the same way he treated them.

Joe looked at his new life as a businessman, owning his own store, as a great stroke of luck but we all figured he earned it by being everybody's friend.

He made his own luck.

The president talked about the stream of illegal immigrants pouring across the nation's border. What this country would have to do to harbor this ever growing number of Spanish-speaking people. I could only think back to how Mexican Joe would have answered.

He would say, "Mister President, those people coming from Mexico who worked hard in the old country will also work hard and try to get ahead and be the good citizens of their new country. Those who would not work in the old country and came to America looking for the good life without working, won't work to get ahead or be good citizens in their new country either."

That's what he would have said had he been given the chance to speak his gratitude to the president of this country he loved with such fervor. Joe seemed to have a knack for getting to the heart of the matter and could brush away the superfluous stuff that most of us get hung up on.

Chapter Twenty Seven - Selling The International

Do what you can, with what you have, where you are. Theodore Roosevelt

The world is changing, and we have to change and adapt.

For most of the crew who had been skinners at the International, some steady, some off and on for many years, it was like home. The closest thing to a real home they had. A place where they would meet real friends, people who cared about them, people who asked about them when they disappeared for a few days now and again.

The International was more than a job; it was a place to seek self-image and self-worth, a place where you were judged by your coworkers on what you did, not on where you came from, or what you had done with your life in the past.

If you had a relapse, fell off the wagon and disappeared for a few days no one sat in judgment when you returned. More likely they would make a joke about you going on a cruise to the Caribbean for a few days. Even Frank the Boss would be glad to see you and would welcome you back.

He treated the skinners who came and went through his company as if they were family and always seemed to be genuinely concerned about them. When someone came in after a week end or week long binge he would send them to The Palace and Lilly would get them fed, showered, clothed and would let them sleep it off, until they were ready to go back on the street.

That's why it came as a surprise when Frank stepped into the bull session one morning and told the crew he was planning on selling the company.

What a bombshell. You could see the shock on the faces and feel the tension in the air, the feeling of disbelief.

For me it wouldn't make a great deal of difference. I was about to finish school and had already passed the FCC tests required for my new job.

I was ready to become a radio announcer and engineer.

Not so with the others. Here was a group of men who had become dependent on Frank the Boss and Lilly at The Palace to pull them through the tight spots and suddenly it was going to end. What would happen if a big company took over?

Some of them would do fine, but for some, the safety net would be gone. They would be faced with producing a set amount of production each day like some of the other large companies required.

They would work for people who didn't care a hoot about their personal problems and would keep them on the job as long as they did the job. If they fouled up they would be gone.

That was the thought in many minds. You could see it in their faces.

Frank saw it too, and explained. His health had been going downhill and his doctor said he should retire and take it a little easier.

Lilly had sold The Palace. He would sell the International. They were going to be married and move to Florida.

There it was bombshell number two. The Palace and Miss Lilly would no longer be there for them either.

No one seemed able to look at anyone else. Eyes shifted nervously but mainly looked at the floor or the ceiling, not at each other. The easy-going banter of the usual morning bull session was gone, the quiet so loud you could almost hear it.

Joe was first to speak. "Good for you Mister Frank," he said, "Good for you. You and Miss Lilly have helped us all and deserve some time to enjoy each other and a life together. Good for you, Mister Frank, good for you."

As Joe ended his impromptu speech, others found their voices and stepped forward to congratulate the man who had been a father figure to them even though many were nearly as old as he was.

Frank and Miss Lilly were getting married. About time they did most of us thought.

The day's work was soon lined out and each crew left for their assignments. Frank looked as if he was feeling as badly as his employees.

As Jamie and I headed for our truck to begin the morning's run Czech said in a low voice, "Jamie, Herring Choker meet us at the Pig's Eye for coffee before you start your run."

We looked at each other and Jamie, obviously not happy at the thought of delaying his arrival at the AA club, agreed, but only for a quick one, as we had to get started.

At the Pig's Eye, we spotted two of the other trucks parked on the street, and several of the crew members who had walking routes or who normally walked to the building they would be working on were also at the old tavern.

Czech greeted everyone at the door, Clyde, Mexican Joe, Gigolo, Jamie and I, Orbit and a couple of others.

"All right everybody, let's make this short we all have work to do. First, we should all be thinking about something we can do for Frank, after all he's done for us."

There were no arguments forthcoming on that, everyone present had been the recipient of a helping hand from Frank and Miss Lilly at one time or another.

"Second we should be thinking about a wedding present, that they can use when they get moved to Florida."

A wedding present, now that was something that most of the crew members hadn't thought about for years, it would be a new experience to go shopping for something for a couple about to get married. Especially this couple who was so well liked and respected by every man present.

"Third," said Czech, "Frank told us he was looking for someone to buy the International. He didn't say he had sold the company. Most of us feel like we are part of the company and like the company is part of us. We've been together for a long time. There's no one around that could run the International like us and we should talk to Frank about selling it to us."

The looks on the faces of the rest of the crew were something. The thought that they could actually own a business was beyond comprehension for most, or at least was pretty hard to bring into focus.

"Yeah, sounds great," said Clyde," but where do we get the kind of money the International is worth? Ain't a man here with more than enough to get through the week, and some will have to draw a couple of bucks ahead from Frank just to make it through the weekend."

"I've been thinking about it since Frank made his announcement," replied Czech, "and I have no idea how we are going to swing it, but I think we should sit down with Frank tonight and ask him.

He's always been straight with us, and if there's any way it can be done, he'll know how to do it."

Heads began nodding in agreement, yeah let's sit down with Frank, and see if it can be done.

Throughout the day as crews met on the streets, or at lunch counters, the subject of how the moneyless crew could purchase the company was discussed and ideas suggested and turned down. One thing was obvious; the International meant a lot to every man on the crew whether they were steady in their job, or whether they were among the skinners who disappeared occasionally for a binge. It was equally obvious that most had questions about their ability to work for someone other than Frank, or to work at the International without him at the helm.

The thought of the International becoming part of a larger company, maybe even one of the national groups, was not a happy one.

The idea of what the company might be worth came from Jamie while he was cleaning a store front on University Avenue. The store owner next door asked him to clean his windows, too, as long as he was there.

Jamie gave him a price, and it suddenly dawned on him that whenever we picked up extra jobs we sold them to Frank for whatever the first month's revenues would be from the job.

"C'mon Kid, let's go find Czech," he said.

As soon as we finished the job we took off down Robert Street to the building Czech and Clyde had been sent to. Spotting Clyde on the fifth floor of the building Jamie shouted, "Clyde, grab Czech and meet us at the Pig's Eye. I think I've got a way this thing will work."

Ten minutes later the second meeting of the day was underway in the back booth of The Pig's Eye Saloon.

Jamie launched into his idea. "We all pick up side jobs from time to time and we sell them to Frank for whatever they bring in for the month."

"Czech you time the jobs and set the price on them," said Jamie, "why couldn't you take all the job slips, figure up what one month's receipts would be, add a little something to it because the companies been here so long, and we could make that an offer to Frank."

Maybe there's a way we could pay Frank off from the receipts each month. If we all really worked we could pick up new jobs and pay a little more each month."

Well there it was, an idea that had merit. An idea that was simple enough so that each member of the crew, no matter what their business acumen, could understand. Since the company would be run exactly as Frank had always run it, he wouldn't have to worry about getting his money. Someone would have to take Frank's place as the head man and everyone present looked at Czech, who looked embarrassed.

"It might work," he said, "It might. What do you think Clyde?"

"I think" said the big man, "that we could own a window cleaning company if we can get everybody to stick together, and to understand that even though we all owned a share of it Czech would be running the show, and that he wouldn't put up with anything that Frank wouldn't put up with."

"All right," said Czech, "Let's go talk to Frank."

And so it began, what would today be called an employee buyout of the company they worked for. Of course that isn't the way the skinners of the International saw it. They saw a simple and direct way to handle a problem. A method by which they would be able to maintain a lifestyle they had developed through the years. As Czech, Jamie and Clyde laid out the plan for Frank his smile grew wider and wider.

It was apparent that he had been sincerely worried about what would happen to the men he had worked with and carried for so many years.

Here was a plan that would solve his problem and theirs too.

At the bull session that night, Frank explained that he was calling a company meeting and that Czech, Clyde and Jamie were presiding.

The window cleaners looked nervous as Czech called the meeting to order and began, in halting terms, to explain the idea Jamie had come up with.

As he proceeded with the plan, he became more and more animated and as he saw the look of excitement and relief that appeared on faces of his coworkers he became more confident and presented the balance of the plan with firm voice.

You could almost see a leader being born before your eyes as he explained how each person would be responsible to the company even though Frank was no longer there. Each person would be responsible to themselves and their coworkers to make sure each job was done properly. Each member of the crew would also be a salesman trying to find new jobs.

Questions began flying as he finished the announcement of the plan. Several stepped over to shake Jamie's hand for coming up with the idea.

And so it happened, Frank and Miss Lily, at last, were getting what they really wanted, each other.

And the company would be maintained as a safe haven for the current crew and those skinners yet to come, who would be looking for a stopping off place on their way up and off of the skid, or perhaps a haven where they could pause for a moment if they were on their way down to the skid from whatever pinnacle they had been on when their slide began.

Chapter Twenty Eight - The End and the Beginning

*Though no one can go back and make a brand new start,
anyone can start from now and make a brand new ending.*

It was a strange feeling, knowing that in a few days I would be leaving for the Upper Michigan city of Iron Mountain to begin my broadcasting career at WMIQ radio.

This was what Lois and I had worked so hard for.

I would soon be working with a new set of characters, a manager, announcers, engineers, salesmen, and an office staff. I wondered if I would learn as much from them, as I had from the crew of the International.

I would be coming back to visit occasionally, as everyone who left always did, and of course it would be different, but somehow the same.

Frank the Boss would be gone, but Czech, looking older and more serious with his new responsibilities would be there to line out the jobs in the morning bull session. To lend a helping hand to those who would be suffering the effects of a bad night on the town.

The old crew members would step forward with a welcoming "Hi Skinner," and the new ones would wonder about the high mucky muck visitor wearing a suit and tie and would wonder how he could ever have been part of their world.

As I thought back to those last days at the International the President was bringing our news conference to a close.

An aide stood and said "Thank you Mr. President," and the small town reporters, gave him a standing ovation.

Obviously pleased with the results of the meeting he looked back from the door and with a big grin said "Thank you for coming to Washington."

With a friendly wave he was gone.

As the other reporters began filing out I took one last look around the richly paneled room with its big leather chairs and thought how like those last days at the International.

You look forward to and work toward something for months or even years, and wait for it as time passes ever so slowly. Then the event you've waited for comes and quickly passes. It's behind you like all of the other experiences you've had and you wonder whether you can ever go back to being the same person you once were.

It was all blurred together, those days at the International, the years as a reporter at small town radio stations, and now a visit with the President.

From the derelicts on skid row to the high mucky mucks I met in Washington, they were all different, yet the same.

People were just people no matter where they were standing when your paths crossed. Each of them touched you in a way that would never be forgotten, in ways that neither you nor they could understand at the time.

"I've got to call Czech," I thought, "I'll find a pay phone here in the White House and I'll call Czech from right here in this building. Won't that give them something to talk about in the bull session tonight."

Then memories of my last visit to the International came flooding back.

Czech was gone. So was Clyde, Mexican Joe, and many of the others.

It had been twenty five years. There was no going back. Only memories of the past, each one a milepost of hope to guide you along that uncertain road into the future. A future filled with new experiences that are sure to create new memories, as did those in the past.

I was leaving the White House after a news conference with the President of the United States, but like Harry The Cat, in my mind I was still living those old memories.

Memories in which I would always be,
The Herring Choker,
Skinner at The International.

www.ingramcontent.com/pod-product-compliance
Lightning Source LLC
Chambersburg PA
CBHW051549280626
47162CB00021B/1652